Back to the Bright Before

Back to the Bright Before

Katherin Nolte

RANDOM HOUSE 🏠 NEW YORK

Text copyright © 2023 by Katherin Nolte
Jacket art and interior illustrations copyright © 2023 by Jen Bricking
Jacket lettering copyright © 2023 by Sarah J. Coleman
Additional interior art used under license by Shutterstock

All rights reserved. Published in the United States by Random House Children's Books, a division of Penguin Random House LLC, New York.

Random House and the colophon are registered trademarks of Penguin Random House LLC.

Visit us on the Web! rhcbooks.com

Educators and librarians, for a variety of teaching tools, visit us at RHTeachersLibrarians.com

Library of Congress Cataloging-in-Publication Data
Name: Nolte, Katherin, author.
Title: Back to the bright before / Katherin Nolte.
Description: First edition. | New York: Random House, [2023] | Audience: Ages 8–12 | Summary: When eleven-year-old Perpetua promises to save her family from financial ruin, she sets off on a quest with her younger brother, a stolen horse, and a chicken in search of a valuable coin.
Identifiers: LCCN 2022013634 (print) | LCCN 2022013635 (ebook) | ISBN 978-0-593-56510-0 (trade) | ISBN 978-0-593-56511-7 (lib. bdg.) | ISBN 978-0-593-56512-4 (ebook)
Subjects: CYAC: Lost and found possessions—Fiction. | Adventure and adventurers—Fiction. | Brothers and sisters—Fiction. | Family life—Fiction. | LCGFT: Novels.
Classification: LCC PZ7.1.N6375 Bac 2023 (print) | LCC PZ7.1.N6375 (ebook) | DDC [Fic]—dc23

The text of this book is set in 12-point Sabon LT Pro.
Interior design by Michelle Crowe

Printed in the United States of America
10 9 8 7 6 5 4 3 2 1
First Edition

Back to the Bright Before

Chapter 1

I **didn't scream when Daddy fell from the ladder.**
My mouth opened, my throat became tight, but I
was as silent as our woodpile when his body tumbled
to the earth. And he did tumble—like an acrobat, end
over end, his giant form arcing in slow motion toward
the ground.

"Impossible," Momma said later, when she asked
me to tell every single detail of what had happened.
"People don't fall in slow motion from the sky."

But he did.

I saw him. I'm eleven years old, which, trust me, is
old enough to know fact from fiction.

"Unbelievable," said Momma when I told her how,
right before he hit the ground, his body straightened

into a horizontal line and floated like a feather. "Two-hundred-pound men don't drift like feathers when they fall."

"Well, Daddy did," I said. "I saw him."

Momma gripped her coffee cup. She was sitting at the kitchen table. Mascara was smudged around her eyes because she'd been crying. It was midnight. Simon was in bed. I should have been in bed, too.

"Get out of here, Pet," she said, voice shaking. "Your lies are making me want to smack you."

I will tell you three things. My name is Perpetua. I do not tell lies. And I was very much happy to oblige.

"That must have been a horrifying experience" is what Sister Melanie said when I told her about Daddy's fall—which was much better than being told you were an impossible, unbelievable liar.

"Do you believe me?" I asked after describing how first he tumbled, then he floated before hitting the ground. It was always hard to tell what Sister Melanie was thinking. She spoke carefully, like each word cost her a nickel and she only had a few quarters in her pocket.

"Of course."

I looked at her. She was the youngest nun in the convent, only twenty, and she had long black hair that she wore in two braids, and equally dark eyes. On her pale face was a pair of bright red glasses.

"I didn't think nuns could wear red" is what Momma had said when I told her about Sister Melanie's glasses.

"Why not?" I asked.

"It has to be against one of their rules. They've got a whole dictionary's worth of them." Momma waved her bottle of glass cleaner dismissively. She was dusting the TV. Simon always smudged it because he thought he could feel people's hair if he ran his fingers across the screen. He never could, of course, but he kept on trying just the same.

My momma doesn't know much about nuns—and that's not an insult. Just a fact. She's never walked down the gravel road with Simon and me to visit the abbey, so why she thought there was a rule against nuns wearing red glasses was anybody's guess.

I didn't try to correct her, though, because she was in one of her moods, and the look on her face as she scrubbed at that TV screen was one baby step shy of furious.

There was a part I left out when Momma asked me to tell her second by second how my daddy fell. I didn't lie about what happened, but what I did was start the telling after the most critical detail. I didn't tell this fact to Sister Melanie, either. That's because I'm proud—not of what happened—no, most certainly not—but just . . . proud. I'm smart. I can do one hundred multiplication problems in one minute, twenty-eight seconds—the fastest in my class. I'm strong. I carried Simon home from the nuns once, when he fell and scraped his shin and made a big show about not walking home, plopping down, toad-like, in the middle of the road. Well, I swung Toad Boy onto my back and carried him the three-quarters of a mile to our fence. I'm tall, which is good for reaching things, and I'm skinny, which makes slipping through cracks easy. I love my freckles and my long hair—strawberry-blond, everyone calls it.

So, see, I'm proud—and when you're proud and you make a giant mistake, you don't want anyone to know. When you're proud, failure is the bitterest fruit you can bite.

That's why I didn't tell Momma or Sister Melanie what I did. But I'm going to tell you.

Some of what happens in this story might seem unbelievable. The things Simon and I saw, what we did, what we found—you might wonder if it's really true.

That's why it's important you believe me. You have to know in the hot, beating center of your heart that Perpetua Martin doesn't lie.

So here goes.

It was my fault Daddy fell from the ladder. His getting hurt—and everything that came after—was all because of me.

It was a Saturday in November. The sun was shining. The air was warm. The wind was whirling leaves into miniature tornadoes. Daddy was cleaning the gutters on our farmhouse. I had the camera Nana sent me from California. It was two days past my birthday, and I was itching to try it out.

"Daddy, look down here," I called up to him. Simon was beside me, of course. He's always beside me, like a piece of gum that no matter how much you scrape, you can't get off the sole of your shoe.

"Hold your horses, Pet," Daddy said in his big, booming voice. Everything about my daddy was big— his six-and-a-half-foot body, his dark, bushy beard, the waves in his hair. "Your dad looks like a lumberjack," kids at school said, trying to be mean, but I always took it as a compliment.

"Please," I cried, "just for a second—look. I want to take your picture." I haphazardly pointed the camera up at him. Really, I had no idea how to use the thing. It was fancy, with a big flash on top and a lens almost as long as a telescope.

"Ridiculous," Momma had said when the camera arrived in the mail. "To send a child a five-hundred-dollar camera. What was she thinking?"

There was a note in the box, on a square of scalloped ivory-colored stationery:

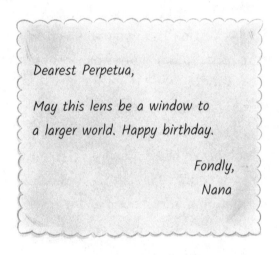

Dearest Perpetua,

May this lens be a window to a larger world. Happy birthday.

Fondly,
Nana

I had never seen or even spoken to my nana. Nobody in my family had since before I was born. She was my sole living grandparent, but she was so absent, she might as well have been a ghost. Except on birthdays. Every year, she sent Simon and me an expensive gift with a cryptic phrase on a piece of scalloped stationery. Her extravagance annoyed Momma to no end. Daddy didn't care, though. He never let Nana bother him.

"Say cheese," I said to Daddy, atop his ladder. "Say cheese, please."

Then Simon picked it up. "Cheese, please! Please, cheese!" he cried like a parrot.

Finally, Daddy looked. He turned his head, high above me, and even though he was so far away, up against the pale November sky, I could see his smile.

"Cheese!" he boomed, his voice a cannon blast.

And that's when that awful wind whipped, the ladder tipped, and Daddy began to somersault through the air.

Chapter 2

Simon didn't talk after that, which was a shame because I had taught him some pretty cool words. Even though he was only four, he could say *indubitably, exuberance,* and *ex nihilo.* (And because I want to prove to you that I don't lie, I'll tell you this: That last part is Latin, and I only know it because Sister Melanie taught it to me.)

So Simon turned silent—except for one word. One word he said in reply to everything. *Cheese.*

Sometimes it was appropriate, like when I asked, "Simon, what would you like to eat?"

"Cheese."

Sometimes it was annoying, like when I said, "Simon, pick a number between one and ten."

"Cheese."

And sometimes it was ridiculous. "Simon, what would you like for Christmas?"

"Cheese."

At first, Momma thought it would pass. "He's just upset is all," she said, smoothing his dark hair off his forehead as she tucked him into bed.

"Cheese," Simon said from beneath his dinosaur sheet, as if agreeing with her.

But as the months went by, and Daddy remained all broken in bed, and the only sound that ever came out of my brother's mouth was a six-letter word from the dairy case, she got worried.

"What a mess," she'd mutter when she got home from a double shift at Carlton's. Momma was a waitress. With Daddy in bed, unable to work, she had started waiting tables from breakfast till close, trying to make up the difference. By the end of the night, her feet were as swollen as balloons. "What a big, fat, giant mess."

She looked at the house, at the dishes in the sink, the toys on the floor, the stack of bills on the table. Yes, the house was a mess. But she meant more than that, too.

"I'll fix it," I told her. It was way past my bedtime. I should have been asleep hours earlier, but Momma had stopped noticing things like bedtimes after Daddy fell. So I stayed up late because I could get away with it.

Momma snapped her head around, quick and angry as a snake. "How are you going to fix it, Pet? Huh? What on earth could you possibly do to fix everything that's wrong?"

I shrugged. "I'll just fix it."

"Great. Good to know, Little Miss Fix-It. Well, you can start with your brother. Teach him to say something besides *cheese*." She stormed out of the kitchen, her reddish-blond ponytail swinging behind her.

Momma was often mean and short-tempered now, but she hadn't always been that way. The two of us used to have the most fun together, especially in her garden. You know how some people have a green thumb? Well, my momma had a whole green hand. She could grow anything with water, sun, and a little bit of patience.

Her garden, let me tell you, was my favorite place to be. Back behind the house, the two of us would work, three seasons out of four. In the spring, I'd help her plant; all summer we'd crawl on our hands and knees, fighting weeds and picking produce; in the fall, when the harvest was over, we'd spread mulch; and winter would find us side by side at the kitchen table, studying seed catalogs and dreaming of next year. Yes, I was Momma's right-hand girl.

How I wish you could have seen it: everything so bright and green, row after row. Kohlrabi, lettuce, strawberries, carrots, potatoes, onions, cantaloupes, pumpkins. My momma grew them all. And I helped her, every step of the way.

But then Daddy fell, and that winter when I showed Momma the seed catalog that had come in the mail, she wouldn't even look at it.

"Not this year, Pet," she said, and shook her head.

"But, Momma," I said, "we've got to *plan*. Spring will be here before you know it."

We were in the kitchen. Momma turned her face toward the window, with its view of the backyard, where her garden lay, brown and bare. "I don't have time anymore. Besides, something tells me spring is a season of the past."

So we didn't plan. And we didn't plant. Instead of having peas from our own yard, we ate them micro-waved from a can. That big rectangle out back, which used to be a living, breathing garden, just sat there, un-loved and dead.

I tried not to look in its direction.

And now, instead of being Momma's right-hand girl, I was just a bother. No matter what I did or said, it was wrong. I was always in her way. But I didn't hold it against her. She deserved to be mad at me. It was all my doing: her aching feet and Daddy's busted body. All because of me and my camera.

Mea culpa.

That's some more Latin that Sister Melanie taught me. It means "my fault."

I am guilty.

Chapter 3

'll tell you how I met Sister Melanie, since you're probably curious. I know it's kind of unusual for an eleven-year-old to be friends with a nun.

Well, I met her at the start of last summer, before Daddy fell. School was out, and I was walking down the gravel road, kicking up dirt and looking for toads, with nothing very interesting to do.

That's when I saw a teenager planting flowers by the side of the road. She had on blue jeans, a bandanna, and red glasses. I stopped to watch her.

After she'd finished digging the hole she was working on, she set down her spade and looked up at me. *"Salve."*

"What does that mean?" I asked.

"It means 'hello,'" she said. "It's Latin."

"Oh. I've never met anyone who speaks Latin."

The teenager laughed. "Neither have I."

"Why are you planting flowers here?" I asked.

"This is where I live," she said.

"On the side of the road?"

"No. *Here.*" She pointed at the metal sign behind her that said *Our Lady of Perpetual Help Abbey.*

Now, I have to tell you, I'd seen that sign my whole life, but that was the first time I actually *saw* it, with my mind and not just my eyes.

"My name's on there," I said, sort of aghast.

"Really?" said the teenager.

"I'm Perpetua."

"Then you are perpetually Perpetua. How exquisite." She stood up and offered me her dirt-covered hand. "I'm Sister Melanie."

"Are you a *nun*?" I know I sounded shocked, which is rude, but I'd never actually seen one of the nuns before. It was kind of like meeting a fairy.

"God willing." She picked up her spade and the empty plastic flower containers. "Perpetua, I must be going, but it was a pleasure to make your acquaintance."

"Wait." I didn't want her to leave just yet. "What's the word you said, that means 'hello'?"

"*Salve,*" said Sister Melanie.

"*Salve*," I repeated. I liked how it felt, kind of mysterious, on my tongue.

Sister Melanie must have known what I was thinking. "I could teach you some Latin, Perpetua, if you'd like."

"I'd like it very much," I said.

Sister Melanie smiled. "Then come back tomorrow, and we shall commence. *Vale*, Perpetua."

"Goodbye, Sister Melanie." I skipped off down the road, pleased to have figured out what *vale* meant.

So that's how it started: both my friendship with Sister Melanie and my love of Latin. Every week, she taught me a new phrase, and I spent the next seven days letting it roll around in my head. Once I'd known her for a year, that meant I could say fifty-two things.

Fifty-two might seem like a lot, but really, it's only the beginning when you think about all the things in the world that must be said.

One of the things that must be said concerns my daddy. He's an artist, I'll have you know. Not the kind you find in a museum, but the kind you find at a fair. He's a woodcutter. He makes sculptures with a chain saw.

They fill our yard, his creations. Most of the statues are bigger than Simon. Some are as tall as I am. There's a fisherman and a grizzly bear, a bald eagle and a tiger. Sometimes people driving past our house see them and stop and buy one. That doesn't happen often, though, out in the country. Daddy makes most of his money in the summer, traveling to the county fairs.

All spring he works in the yard, wearing goggles and headphones, his big red chain saw humming. After school, Simon and I watch him. We've each got our own pair of headphones, but the chain saw is so loud that it makes our bones buzz, even with them on. We have to keep our distance because of the flying wood chips. It's almost magic, the way my daddy can turn an old tree stump into something wonderful—cut by cut, slice by bone-buzzing slice.

The fairs pay him to give demonstrations, and he sets up a display of his statues. Last year, I was old enough to go with him to the different fairgrounds. I got to hear the crowds *ooh* and *aah* as they tried to guess what he was turning the blocks of wood into. I also helped run his store, pointing out the wooden details to customers: the curve of the turtle's shell, each flame in the Statue of Liberty's torch.

Daddy sold one hundred statues last year—his most

ever. Momma was so proud. I don't know how she did it, but she baked him a cake shaped like a tree, with green and brown frosting. Simon couldn't stop laughing when Daddy cried "Timber!" and used a knife to chop it down.

The next day, Daddy carved a new statue, but this one wasn't for sale. It was of a man, a woman, a girl, and a little boy. All of them were stacked on top of each other, with the man at the top and his arms reaching down past the woman and the girl, encircling everyone, including the boy at the bottom. We put it on the front porch and stood admiring it as the sun began to set and the first lightning bugs flashed hello.

We were so happy then. Life was bright and sweet, and it felt like that's how it was going to be forever.

It was my daddy's shoulder that got the worst of it when he fell, but also his leg. "You're lucky you didn't die," the doctor told him.

I remembered him floating, hanging for those few moments between *caelum et terra*. Heaven and earth. Despite what Momma said, I knew that impossible, unbelievable fact is what saved him.

But Daddy didn't feel lucky. He felt bitter. Though his broken leg healed, his knee never felt right, and every other step made him wince. And his shoulder— that was a whole different sort of weight to bear. The muscle detached when he hit the ground. We spent the money from the one hundred statues to fix it. But the surgery didn't work. So Daddy had another surgery, despite our not having the money to pay for it. That surgery failed, too.

Momma wanted him to try again. "Third time's a charm, isn't that right?" she said, attempting to sound hopeful, even though her eyes were as flat and unbelieving as stones.

"No. I'm done wasting money we don't have," Daddy said defiantly from his bed. His right arm hung limp and useless at his side. "I'm done digging a hole we're never going to get out of."

"So this is your new life?" Momma asked, her voice

chipped with panic. "You're just going to sit in bed with that empty look on your face?"

"I suppose so," he said.

We tried to make him change his mind, but it's like that spark that makes a person want to try had been snuffed out of Daddy when he fell from the sky.

The thing we all knew, though none of us dared say, was that if he didn't get his shoulder fixed, he couldn't be an artist anymore. No way on earth could a man operate a chain saw one-handed. Daddy knew this, which in a mixed-up, backward way is why he didn't want to have another surgery. He didn't want to get his hopes up. He didn't want to imagine the smell of sawdust and the feel of wood yielding beneath his hands, only to have the operation fail again. Daddy was too scared to believe in something better.

"Fear can paralyze a person," Sister Melanie told me. "Turn blood into stone."

Maybe, I thought, my daddy just needed a reminder of how it had been, how it could be if he'd try again. So I got the last statue he'd carved, the four of us all stacked up. It was much too heavy to carry, so I tipped it into Simon's red wagon and pulled it from the front porch into the house. I pulled it through the kitchen and the living room and into my daddy's room, where the curtains were drawn and it always seemed dark, even when the sun was shining.

I didn't look at him. Sometimes it was just too hard to. The longer he stayed in bed, the smaller he got somehow. It's not something a girl likes to see, the months passing, and her daddy shrinking, and the light surrounding him all faded and gray. I stopped the wagon at the foot of his bed and stood the wooden statue upright. Finally, I met his gaze.

"Lookee here," I cried, puffing out my chest, like the proudest of peacocks. "Look what my daddy made."

He looked. Long and hard, he studied that carving. For a second, I thought it was coming back to him: the buzz of the blade, the creator he had been, the creator he could still be. But then his eyes flashed angrily.

"Get it out of here!" he yelled. "Get it out!"

His voice. I'd never heard it so loud. It rattled the windowpanes. It made my ears ring. Quickly I pulled the wagon into the hallway. And that's when I knew how really broken everything was. My daddy—my big, strong lumberjack daddy—was afraid. He was so afraid of what had happened in the past that he wouldn't let his heart have hope for the future.

I took the wagon back outside, returned the statue to its rightful place on the front porch. Then I made a resolution: I would be brave, if Daddy could not. I would put my faith in a future filled with fairs and the sweet scent of sawdust. I would fix all the problems that stupid camera and I had caused.

All I had to figure out was how to do it.

Chapter 4

What's the one thing that would convince Daddy to have another surgery?" I asked.

"Cheese," said Simon.

We were walking down the road, headed to visit Sister Melanie at the abbey. It was June fifteenth, Simon's fifth birthday. Momma was scheduled to work till closing at Carlton's, and Daddy, I knew, would sit in doomed dreariness in his bedroom. So it was up to me to make Simon's birthday special.

I know I compared him to a piece of chewed-up bubble gum earlier, so I would like to clarify those remarks. See, if my brother were a piece of gum, he'd be the best flavor: grape, with a sweet, juicy center. I liked Simon an awful lot. I guess because he was my baby brother.

He was dark where I was light. He took after Daddy where I favored Momma. Dark brown eyes and hair, pudgy body with a round little belly, and the sweetest circular face. Momma said one day Simon would grow up to be even bigger than Daddy, which was hard to believe. I thought he looked like something a baker would make: a perfect little gingerbread boy for sale in a display case. Sometimes I called him Cookie Boy because of this.

Well, I made Cookie Boy a felt crown for his birthday, which I gave him after a breakfast of cinnamon toast. Now he was wearing this crown and holding a stick with a knobby bulb on the end that I'd found in the backyard and painted gold to look like a scepter. I held his other hand. The day was warm and sunny, the second week of summer vacation, and dandelions dotted the ditch.

"That's right," I said, pretending Simon had said something reasonable in reply to my question about Daddy's surgery. "Daddy needs money. If we had plenty of money, he wouldn't be afraid to have another surgery. So here's the next question, Simon. Where can we get some money?"

My brother bit his lip and kicked the gravel road. "Cheese?"

I sighed. I had an awful lot of work to do if the boy

was going to be holding intelligent conversations by the time kindergarten started in August. But I had to put first things first, as Sister Melanie was always saying, and first was money for Daddy's surgery. Even before that, though, was taffy for my brother's birthday.

We'd come to the metal *Our Lady of Perpetual Help Abbey* sign that marked the entrance to where the nuns lived. Without the sign, you'd never guess that out here in the country, in the middle of us normal, everyday folks, a group of nuns owned two hundred acres of rolling valley. They lived all together in a red stone building with a chapel attached to it. They also owned an old farmhouse at the bottom of a winding lane, where people could come and stay for a little peace and quiet.

"Only a fool would pay money to stay in an old farmhouse," Momma said when I told her about it. "I live in an old farmhouse every day, and trust me, it's neither peaceful nor quiet."

"You don't have to pay to stay there," I tried to explain. "It's free."

Momma pulled the vacuum out of the closet and plugged it into the wall. "I'm going to teach you something important, Pet. Nobody gives you anything for free. Not even those sisters."

Now, my momma is the smartest person I know. Smarter, even, than all my teachers. But the nuns were the one thing she couldn't figure out. She and they saw the world through different sets of eyes. Momma's eyes, so keen and clear, saw the world as it was right now. She saw a messy house, a restaurant full of hungry customers, and a hurt husband in his bed. But the nuns, they saw the world as it could be if you moved all the troublesome stuff out of the way. They saw a home built on love, a room filled with souls, and a man with a thousand ideas just waiting to spring from his hands.

Momma didn't hate the sisters. Please don't think that. She just couldn't understand them. And when you can't understand something, it's like you don't see it right, which is why she said things like "Nobody gives you anything for free" even though the nuns gave us free stuff all the time: eggs from their chickens, honey from their beehives, and candy from their sticky hands.

See, the nuns had a motto they followed: *ora et labora*. That means "pray and work." And pray and work was just about all they did. Praying, they did the most of—seven times a day. They even got up in the middle of the night to pray. Regular folks were allowed to watch them, in the guest chapel. Simon and I had gone several times. You sit in pews, and there's a metal gate that separates you from the sisters. There's a stone altar with a candle on it, and a big crucifix hanging from the ceiling. The sisters sing and chant, and they speak very,

very slowly. I mean turtle-tiptoeing-on-ice slow. If you happen to be there for the final prayer of the night, the one the sisters say before they go to bed, the leader of the nuns—the mother superior—will come to the gate with a metal wand and a pail of water. She'll dip the wand in the water and then flick her wrist so it rains all over you and the pews.

Sister Melanie said it's a bedtime blessing, and anyone who receives it will have good dreams. I've only received it once. That night, I dreamed a bad man was chasing me. I had to hide in a cave to try to escape him. It was dark and cold, and I was terribly frightened. But all of a sudden, a little lamb appeared. It climbed on top of a boulder in the middle of the cave and opened its mouth as if to speak. And that's when I woke up, heart thudding in my chest, mind full of wonder about what it meant. If that was a good dream, I'd hate to have a nightmare.

Anyway, the nuns pray, which I guess everybody knows, but they also work. They have a candy factory. It's a wooden building just up the lane from their chapel. They make taffy—little rectangles of chewy, fluffy perfection—that they sell on the internet.

That's what Simon and I were coming for today. Those sweet, sweet taffies. The nuns worked till eleven-thirty in the candy factory, then stopped for lunch and prayer. Simon and I hid behind a blue spruce and waited for them to file out. Sister Melanie would be last. She was a novice, which means "new," so she was the one who always turned out the lights and locked the door.

We watched the sisters walk by. Some were quite old and took shuffling steps. Others had gray hair but were still strong. Sister Melanie looked like a girl compared to the rest, so much younger was she in her red glasses and braids. No matter their age, all the sisters always seemed happy, laughing and talking on their way out of the factory. I told Momma once how joyful they were.

"They're faking, Pet," she said. "No one who has to get up at three o'clock in the morning every day is happy about it."

Maybe Momma was right. But they sure didn't *look* like they were faking. They didn't look like nuns, either, when they came out of the candy factory. Praying, they wore white robes and black veils (except Sister Melanie, whose veil was white since she was a novice). When they worked, though, they dressed like regular people, in blue jeans and T-shirts, with bandannas on their heads. (Which is why I didn't realize Sister Melanie was a nun that first time I met her.)

Finally, Sister Melanie exited the factory. We waited

till she was halfway across the parking lot, then stepped out from behind the tree.

"Perpetua! Simon! *Salvete!*" she cried with delight. That's how she always greeted us, like we were long-lost relatives with whom she'd finally been reunited. Like we were the most important people in the whole world. It made you want to see her whenever you could.

"How are you two this morning?" she asked. She was in her farmer clothes and had a smudge of taffy on her red glasses.

"Very well, thank you," I answered for both of us. I tried to speak in a sophisticated manner when around Sister Melanie. I don't know why, but she made me want to do everything better.

"How is your father?"

I glanced at Simon, in his homemade crown, holding his homemade scepter. I didn't know how much he understood about what was happening in our house. I had to be careful not to frighten him. "Daddy has seen better days," I said after some deliberation.

She nodded solemnly. "I will continue to pray for him."

Now, please don't think I'm greedy. I only said what I said next for Simon's sake. Since he would get no presents—there was no money for presents; there was no money for anything—I wanted him to get something.

"Today is Simon's fifth birthday."

"Well, happy birthday, Simon." Sister Melanie reached into the breast pocket of her T-shirt, pulled out a wax-paper-wrapped taffy, and dropped it into his pudgy hand.

"Thank you very much," I said. Then I cleared my throat a little and added, "Simon, unfortunately, will have no party."

"Oh, that's too bad." Sister Melanie put her hands on her denim knees and bent down so she could look Simon in the eye. "If you could have any one thing on your birthday, what would it be?"

Simon scrunched up his face like he was really thinking. He crossed his arms and looked toward the sky. Finally, he said, in a dreamy voice, "Cheese."

Sister Melanie laughed.

"He doesn't really want cheese," I hurriedly explained, even though she probably knew that.

Sister Melanie laughed some more. "One moment please," she said, and went back inside the factory.

Simon and I waited. The wind blew warm and lifted the ends of my hair. I'll tell you what I thought about, standing there. It was something I often thought about, turning it over and over, like a pebble, in my mind. Sister Melanie would live right here forever. When I grew up, I might stay in Iowa, or I might move away. I might become an astronaut, or a mother, or the president of the United States. Maybe all three. But no matter where I went or what I did, Sister Melanie would be right here, praying and making taffy. It was like I had a map of her life in my brain that I could carry around forever. When I became worried, I thought about Sister Melanie and how her path was all laid out before her. Then I always felt a little bit better. I don't know why.

"Happy birthday, Simon!" she said when she returned, and she handed him a purple rectangular box with *Our Lady of Perpetual Help Abbey* stamped in gold foil on the top. "Here, let me help you." She carefully lifted the box's lid to reveal row after row of taffy.

Simon's eyes grew wide. "Cheese," he said in the most awestruck manner.

"He means thank you," I said.

"You're quite welcome." Sister Melanie glanced at her watch. "There's twenty minutes till prayer. That's plenty of time for chickens."

Simon jumped up and down. "Cheese! Cheese!"

"Come on," said Sister Melanie. We followed her away from the candy factory and down the hill.

Simon loved the nuns' chickens. They had a couple dozen, and they were all beauties. Not your typical white chickens—they were red, brown, and gray. Sister Melanie had named them all. Most had human names—Catherine, Agnes, Theresa—but three black-and-white Barred Rocks she'd named Faith, Hope, and Charity. Of these, Hope was the smallest and Simon's favorite. Even though, in her whole chicken life, she'd never laid a single egg.

The birds were located at the bottom of a valley, near the farmhouse you could reserve for retreats. When we reached the henhouse, the chickens were strutting about in the yard, their feathers bright and glorious under the noonday sun. Simon immediately ran to Hope, scooped up her small frame, and pressed his Cookie Boy face into her black-and-white feathers.

Sister Melanie handed out rice for us to cup in our outstretched palms so the chickens would eat from our hands. She went into the henhouse while we fed the greedy birds and came back a few minutes later, holding a wicker basket. "Here," she said, handing me the basket. "Perhaps your mother could make Simon an omelet."

There were a dozen beautiful eggs in the bottom: white, brown, the lightest shade of olive. I didn't have the heart to tell Sister Melanie that Momma would work until Simon went to bed. There would be no omelet today. "Thank you very much," I said. "We do appreciate it."

Sister Melanie looked at me, and all of a sudden her expression changed. It became quite serious and full of concern. "You must be careful," she said quietly as Simon stood a few yards away, snuggling Hope against his chest. A sort of sorrowful smile spread across her face. "You remind me of myself when I was your age."

I nodded, though I wasn't sure what she was saying.

"I'm going to give you something very special." She slipped a hand into the pocket of her jeans and pulled out a small silver saltshaker. She handed it to me. "Here."

"For the omelet?" I asked, confused.

"Oh, Perpetua," she said, shaking her head. "Not for the omelet. This is for when things get bad. When you are in definite danger. You'll know when you need it. Understand?"

I didn't understand and was about to tell her so, when all of a sudden I remembered my dream, the one in which I was being chased by a bad man whom I could not see. And for a moment it was like I stepped outside time, like I was everywhere at once. I was here, right now, with the chickens, but I was also asleep all those weeks ago, in my bed. Plus, I was in a future filled with fear, clutching the silver saltshaker.

A shiver ran through me.

"Promise you'll keep it with you."

"I promise," I said, and slipped it into my pocket.

Simon was coming toward us, carrying his chicken. I had the eggs in one hand, taffies in the other. Both felt impossibly heavy.

"Be careful," Sister Melanie murmured, so quiet I could hardly hear her.

I put on a brave smile because I had vowed to, for Daddy. "I'm not afraid," I said, wrapping an arm around my little brother.

I really do hope I wasn't lying.

Chapter 5

Next, we visited Mr. Hollis. Because Simon could not have a party, I was creating one for him, house by house.

Now, Mr. Hollis, whom everyone called Holly, was not the sort of person most would invite to a birthday party, not even a traveling party, like ours. He was unfriendly, sour, pessimistic to his bones. "A crooked root of an old man" is what Momma called him. "Never performed an act of kindness in his life. Never spoke a word that wasn't bathed in bitterness."

I'm not one to make excuses for people, even though Sister Melanie says we should. She says we should think of all the reasons somebody might act unpleasantly so we can walk a mile in their shoes. Well, I had no interest in wearing Holly's old, mud-caked boots, but I will tell you why he acted so horribly: He was lonely. His wife was dead, and he had no children. It was just him, day after day, on his little ramshackle farm. Just him.

And the ponies.

The ponies, of course, were why we visited him.

There were four of them, though there used to be six. Two had died during the winter, and Holly had dug a tractor-size hole behind the barn to bury them.

The ones that remained were almost magical. Smaller than me, with big glassy eyes and muzzles as soft as peaches—Simon and I loved to go into the barn and visit them. Sometimes Holly would pay us to help muck their stalls. We loved those little ponies. They were creatures from a far-off, miniature planet. Their names were as precious as they were: Crystal, Ruby, Emerald, and Diamond. Crystal was our favorite.

Once upon a time, the ponies had made Holly happy, but now, like everything else, they only made him bitter. See, the old man had had a business. Holly's Happy Horses it was called. You could pay to come and ride the ponies on the weekend. His wife sold all sorts of homemade cookies and cakes. There was a gift shop inside a shed, filled with souvenirs: plastic ponies, key chains, cups. Holly's was a regular tourist attraction, out here in the country. People on their way to someplace else would stop and spend twenty dollars, just so their kids could tell their classmates they'd been there.

Then times changed. Holly's wife died. There were no more cakes and cookies. Children lost interest in ponies. Instead, they watched TV or played video games. The business closed when I was a toddler. And Holly had been grumpy ever since.

"Now, don't mind him if he says something rude," I told Simon. We'd come to Holly's driveway. I set the basket of eggs and box of taffies in the grass. "Remember: that's just the way he is."

Simon nodded solemnly, and his crown slipped down over his eyes.

I helped him fix it. "Okay. Now we're ready. Here we go."

Holly's house was falling apart. The shutters were all dangling or disappeared, the paint was peeling, and the roof shingles were standing up on end. "Haunted" is what some kids on the school bus called it. But it wasn't haunted, just given-up on.

We walked past the falling-apart house to the barn,

where Holly was sitting on an overturned five-gallon bucket.

"Good morning," I called.

"Says who?" he said gruffly. He was tall and bony with thin gray hair. On his wide face he wore a perpetual frown.

"It's Simon's birthday," I told him.

Holly grunted, unimpressed. "How old is ya?"

"Cheese," Simon said.

"Three?" Holly asked. "You're awful big for three. You might grow up to be a giant, the rate you're going."

"He's five," I interjected.

"Then why'd he say three?"

"He didn't say three. He said *cheese*."

"Well, cheese ain't a number." Holly eyed us suspiciously.

The thing about Holly was, he didn't really say much, which made visiting difficult. I had to think up all the topics of conversation, and then wait and see if he'd offer a reply.

"What's a good way to get money?" I asked, because that's what was on my mind. I needed money for Daddy's surgery so he could use his chain saw again.

"Rob a bank," Holly said.

"A *nice* way to get money," I clarified.

Holly was silent, staring at the pony stalls across from him. I could smell the ponies and hear the clip of their hooves and the swish of their tails, but I couldn't see them, not yet. If I wanted to see the ponies, I had to woo the grumpy gatekeeper first.

"Now, why would you think I'd know a thing about makin' money? Do I look like a rich man?"

"No, sir."

"That was a stupid question, then, wasn't it?"

I clenched my fists. There was nothing I hated more than being called that word. That word made me want to punch and kick. But I had to get to the ponies, for Simon, so I gritted my teeth and said, "Yes."

Holly looked at Simon. "Is your sister always that stupid?"

"Cheese," Simon said, which I like to think meant, "My sister is the smartest girl in all of Iowa. If you insult her again, I'll karate chop your head."

"What did you say?" Holly asked, but then seemed to notice Simon's crown for the first time. "What's that awful-lookin' thing on your head?"

"It's a crown," I said proudly. The crown looked splendid, perfectly regal. Holly calling it awful did not make it so, and I would not pretend otherwise. "I made it. For his birthday."

"Birthday, eh?" Holly massaged his knees with his

big, gnarled hands. "Don't know why there always has to be such a fuss about birthdays. Everybody—unless they're dead—gets old." He looked at me with eyes that were cold and sad. "I suppose he wants to see the ponies."

"Yes, sir."

Holly gestured toward the stalls. "Go on."

I took Simon by the hand and led him across the barn. One by one, we peered at the ponies. Simon was perched on my hip so he could have a good view. There was Diamond, brownish red with a mane to match, munching hay from her feeder. Next, we saw Ruby and Emerald, the dappled-gray twins. They stood in their stalls, swishing their tails to keep the flies away. We saved Crystal for last. White with a blond mane and eyes that were icy blue, she was a sight to behold. Looking at that pony made you remember the world was grand and mysterious.

Crystal stood perfectly still in her stall, a living statue, and gazed at us.

"Cheese," Simon breathed in admiration from his spot on my hip.

"She's beautiful, isn't she?" I agreed.

Some days Holly let us go into the stalls to touch them. Others, he'd get the ponies out and they'd prance in a corralled section of his yard. His mood today, though, seemed particularly foul, so I knew both of those options were out of the question.

What I did not know, standing and admiring the alabaster pony, was that I was living my last moments as an innocent.

See, in less than twenty-four hours, I would steal her.

Chapter 6

Simon and I headed back down the road, past our own house and to the property that lay to the north. This was the residence of Mrs. Marianne Minnow, a widow who kept her home as tidy as Holly's was neglected.

She lived in a yellow cottage with white shutters and displayed a big, bushy wreath on the front door, which changed with the seasons. Inside, her house was full of flowers, shiny mirrors, and framed pictures. Every time we visited, she gave us each a bag of vanilla wafer cookies. That's why we were visiting today. I wanted the cookies. Another gift for Simon.

I set the eggs and taffies on the front steps and

knocked on the door. Mrs. Minnow appeared, holding a photo album.

"Oh dear. It's Perpetua and Simon," she said, opening the door to let us in. Her hair was cut in a red bob. She always wore lipstick and nail polish. Mrs. Minnow was what my momma called a "professional worrier." If there was something to think about and get worked up over, Mrs. Minnow would do it. Every other sentence that came out of her mouth contained the phrase "oh dear."

"Today is Simon's birthday," I told her. We stepped into the front room, which had lace curtains and smelled like potpourri. "He's five."

"Oh dear. Happy birthday."

"Cheese," Simon said happily.

Fortunately, Mrs. Minnow was slightly hard of hearing.

"I was just going through some old photo albums. Would you two like to join me?"

"That sounds lovely." I always tried to speak in a soothing manner around Mrs. Minnow, hoping to ease her worried mind.

"Oh dear. I almost forgot. There are two garbage bags full of cans in the garage."

"How kind of you to save them for us," I said.

Momma could get a nickel a can at the grocery store, so Mrs. Minnow had been collecting them for us ever since Daddy's fall. Maybe you think, *Two garbage bags is a lot of pop for one woman to drink*. Well, they weren't pop cans. They were beer. And Mrs. Minnow didn't drink them. Her son did. But I won't talk about Gordon just yet.

Mrs. Minnow sat down in the middle of her couch. Simon and I sat on either side of her. "Oh dear," she said, and opened the album on her lap.

The pictures were black and white, a little fuzzy. "Here I am as a baby," she said, pointing a purple fingernail at one of the photos. She proceeded to lead us page by page through her life. To be honest, it was not the most interesting way to pass an hour. My mind began to wander. I thought of Daddy with his broken arm and broken spirit, tired of trying, in his bed.

"What's the best way to get rich?" I interrupted, which was very rude, I admit.

"Oh dear. I don't know anything about getting rich," Mrs. Minnow said. She looked back down at the pictures of herself from long ago. "It's funny, though, that you should ask. . . ."

Have you ever known that what a person was about to say would change everything? Have you ever sat with your heart beating wildly in your chest, as if waiting for the curtain to rise on a theatrical show? That's how it was for me. I stared at Mrs. Minnow with her red hair and purple fingernails, and it was like I could hardly breathe.

"When I was a girl," she began, "I used to hunt for a treasure. You know the abbey down the road?"

Simon and I nodded eagerly.

"Oh dear. Well, when I was young, we were convinced that a monk had hidden a rare and valuable coin there."

"Where?" I asked.

Mrs. Minnow laughed. "If we knew, we would've found it, wouldn't we? No, we weren't sure where. All we had was the poem."

"Poem?"

"Let me see. Oh dear." Mrs. Minnow closed her eyes, trying to remember. "My father taught it to me:

> "Harden not your heart
> That is the place to start
> Enchantment is advancement
> Fear will draw you near
> Though the cave be dark and dreary
> Little ones won't grow weary
> When upon the rock they find
> The coin that leads to peace of mind"

"Say it again," I begged.

Mrs. Minnow recited the poem more confidently the second time.

"Is there a cave at the abbey?" I asked.

"If there is, we never found it. We kids used to flock there after school, searching. We'd bring flashlights, ropes, matches." She gave a nervous laugh. "It got so bad the nuns had to keep guard at the fence line and shoo us away. Oh dear."

"How long did you search?" I wanted to know.

"Oh, a couple of years, at least."

"Why did you stop?"

Mrs. Minnow studied her photo album again. "Hoping for things that don't materialize eventually becomes too heavy a weight to carry."

I was about to ask another question when a voice said, "I never heard you talk about no hidden treasure."

The three of us froze on the couch.

"Oh dear," Mrs. Minnow murmured.

Gordon, her wayward son, stood in front of us. He wore ripped-up blue jeans and a black T-shirt that had been washed so many times it was almost gray. He had unkempt gray hair, long, furry sideburns, and sharp amber eyes.

Though they were the same age, Daddy and Gordon couldn't be more different. While Daddy was big

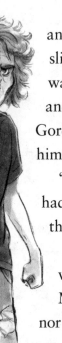

and powerful, like a lion, Gordon was slight and mangy, like a wolf. Daddy was a maker—he could take something and turn it into something else—while Gordon created only messes, for both himself and everyone around him.

"You beware of Gordon," Momma had warned me. "That man is bad through and through."

But to avoid Gordon completely would mean no longer visiting Mrs. Minnow, which seemed neither just nor right. I had to be careful around him, was all. *Cave canem,* you know? Beware of the dog. Or, in this case, the wolf.

"Why didn't you ever tell me about the hidden treasure?" Gordon tried again.

Mrs. Minnow was a little scared of him, you could tell. Her hands fluttered about in her lap like frightened birds. "There is no treasure. It was just a game I played as a child."

Gordon crossed his wiry arms. "Then why are you telling these kids how to find it?"

Gordon said the word *kids* the way Momma said *maggots.* He hated Simon and me. You could feel the hate oozing from his body.

"All I'm telling them is a poem I memorized long ago." Mrs. Minnow stood up. "It's probably time for you to leave," she said to me. "I'll get you your vanilla cookies."

We followed her into the kitchen, Gordon's angry eyes boring holes in my back. Mrs. Minnow counted out six cookies into two sandwich bags. Then she handed them to us and leaned down close by my ear. "I hope you find it," she whispered. Then loudly she said, "Don't forget the cans in the garage."

I nodded and took Simon by the hand. I led him past Gordon without even looking in that bad man's direction. Then we were on the porch, and I had just picked up the basket of eggs, when the screen door slammed behind us.

"Don't think I don't know what you're up to," Gordon said, walking toward me, slow and steady. "You come here, take my food, take my cans. Well, there's no way I'm letting you take my treasure."

I stepped backward. "I don't want your treasure," I said, and that was not a lie. Gordon didn't own a treasure.

"I'm not a nice person," he said, creeping closer, his amber eyes hard and full of hatred. "I'm not like my mother."

I took another step backward, trying to escape him,

and fell off the porch. The basket flew from my hand, and eggs shattered around me.

"Cheese!" Simon cried, racing down the porch steps. He had his box of taffies in his hand.

"There goes the omelet Momma didn't have time to make you," I told my brother when he was beside me on the grass.

Simon clenched his fists and looked up at Gordon. "Cheese!" he screamed. "Cheese, cheese, cheese!" I think he was yelling curse words, though I'm not one hundred percent sure.

Gordon ignored him. "You see those eggs?" he growled, looking right at me and the dozen broken shells. "That's what'll happen to you if you try to take what's mine."

He stormed back inside.

I picked myself up and brushed the dirt off my pants. "Come on, Simon. Let's go get the cans." My voice was shaky, and my ankle hurt where I'd landed on it. I was more sorrowful than words can say about that basket of eggs.

But because I was eleven, I didn't cry.

Chapter 7

I was wrong about Simon not getting any presents. There was a gift-giver whom I forgot. When we returned home, a package was waiting on the front porch from Nana.

Like I said earlier, we never actually saw our nana. She lived in California and had been in a fight with Momma my whole life. There wasn't even a picture of her in our house. I had an image of her in my mind, though. I imagined her with curly blond hair, a diamond necklace, and a fur coat. I asked Momma if that was right, but she wouldn't tell me.

Nana was rich enough that she could have paid for both of Daddy's surgeries, but she didn't. Momma didn't ask her to. See, Momma hadn't talked to Nana in years. Nana had forbidden Momma to marry Daddy, who she thought was a waste of a fellow.

My momma grew up rich, which is hard to imagine. She went to private schools and sailed on cruise ships across the ocean. Daddy, on the other hand, was just a regular guy who did regular things. I'm so glad Momma chose him anyway. He was the most perfect daddy in the world. Until he fell off the ladder.

Simon was very excited to see the package. "Cheese!" he cried, and tried to drag it into the house himself. It was much too big for a five-year-old, so I set down the garbage bags filled with cans and helped him.

We carried it into the living room, and I got some scissors to open it. Inside was a long box wrapped in gold paper and tied with a white ribbon. An envelope was taped on top.

"Open the envelope first," I instructed.

Simon dutifully obeyed. There was the same scalloped stationery Nana always sent. The note said:

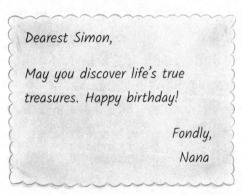

Dearest Simon,

May you discover life's true treasures. Happy birthday!

Fondly,
Nana

I wondered what could be in the package. All the gifts Nana had sent over the years—porcelain dolls, dinosaurs carved from precious stones, the infamous camera—had been sold to pay for Daddy's surgeries. This gift, whatever it was, would be sold, too—which is why I sort of hoped Simon wouldn't like it.

"Let's open it in front of Daddy," I said because I felt sorry for that man, who hid himself away, so ashamed of his brokenness.

Daddy's door was shut, so I knocked, then gently pushed it open. There he was, sitting up in bed, his hair and beard as dark as ever. He didn't read or watch TV, but just sat and looked out the window. I don't know what he thought about all day, but I wondered if he was imagining a different world, one where his arm was healed and he was once again holding a chain saw.

"Good afternoon!" I said as cheerfully as possible. "Would you like to see Simon's present?" Sister Melanie said the world can only be as joyful as the people in it. I tried to be joyful so Daddy could be, too.

"Is it your birthday, Simon?" Daddy asked. His voice was sort of quiet, as if he was astonished by the possibility.

Simon nodded.

"What day is it?"

"June fifteenth," I said.

Daddy turned toward the window and looked out across our yard.

I knew what he was doing. He was calculating how much time had passed since his accident. How many days had been wasted. I hauled Simon's gift onto the bed in order to stop him.

"Here you go, Simon," I said. "Rip it open."

Simon climbed onto the bed and tore at the wrapping paper.

Treasure Hunter Z300, the box said, and under the letters was a picture of a metallic wand.

"What is it?" I asked.

"A metal detector," Daddy said. "If that isn't a strange gift to send a five-year-old . . ."

We all just stared at the box for a minute, and then I helped Simon open the end, so he could pull the metal detector out. There were instructions: *Important! Save me!* the top of the sheet said. I read the whole thing, and then I took Simon outside to search our yard. We found two bottle caps, a zipper, a fork, three pennies, and five nails. Simon was so excited, you'd think he'd found a handful of diamonds. We put all the items in the egg basket and brought them inside to show Daddy.

He took out each one and looked at it, but his eyes, I could tell, weren't really seeing. His body was here, but his mind was someplace else. When he was done, he gave the basket back and said, "Do you remember what I gave you last year for your birthday?"

Now, Simon was only four on his last birthday, so I wasn't sure if he remembered. *I* remembered, though, so I said, "Oh yes! The little dog! Go get it, Simon."

Simon raced off to his room and came back with the wooden dachshund Daddy had made him. My daddy can carve things both big and small. He can use chain saws and also whittling knives.

Simon put the dog in Daddy's palm, and I watched him raise up his good arm so the dog was level with his face. He studied it.

The dachshund was amazing. You could see the holes for its nostrils and the whiskers, thin as floss, protruding from its snout. It looked like the kind of creature in a storybook that a fairy would tap with her wand and bring to life.

Daddy's face changed into a sort of frown, and he wrapped his fingers tightly around the dog. "What did I carve you this year, Simon?" he asked. His voice sounded thick, almost like he was choking.

Daddy didn't carve Simon anything this year, of course. He couldn't because of his arm. I looked at Simon and shook my head, which meant, *Don't say anything.*

"What did I carve you this year?" Daddy asked again.

Sometimes I think it might be cruel to act joyful when somebody you love with your whole heart is upset and in pain. So I stopped trying. And I just said, with sadness in my voice, "Nothing, Daddy."

He blinked and looked at me as if he'd forgotten I was there. "That's right. I didn't carve him anything." His gaze went back to the window, his ruined arm hanging limply at his side. Somehow, he looked more piteous than ever.

Simon's eyes filled with tears.

"I think you best leave now," Daddy said, still looking out the window.

There was a cake mix, but Momma had forgotten to buy frosting, so I made Simon a cake and coated it in powdered sugar. I let him eat it for dinner. Then I gave him three of his taffies from Sister Melanie for dessert. I thought about taking a piece of cake to Daddy, but eating cake alone in bed struck me as the saddest thing ever. So I didn't.

Momma was still at work when eight o'clock rolled around. I put Simon to bed myself. I let him wear his crown and tucked his scepter and metal detector in beside him. I set the basket of found objects and the box of taffies at the foot of his bed.

Pulling the dinosaur sheet up to his chin, I asked, "Did you have a good birthday?"

"Cheese," he said sleepily, a smile on his face.

"Good." I turned on his box fan and turned off his light, then went to the kitchen to wait for Momma.

At the table, alone, I thought about how last year at this time she and I were picking strawberries till the sun went down. Sometimes we'd stay out there so long, Daddy would have to call us in. Yes, a garden was a lot of work, but it was a good kind of work, the kind that made you feel satisfied. Oh, how I missed the hours we used to spend together.

I had fallen asleep when Momma finally got home. She had on her red Carlton's T-shirt and her black waitress pants and black walking shoes. She took one look at me sitting there, with the partially eaten birthday cake, and slumped down in a chair on the other side of the table.

"I can't believe I missed the whole thing." She was crying.

"We could have another party, on your day off," I suggested, though when Momma would ever get a day off, I had no idea. She was working every single shift she could get her hands on. And working in a restaurant, at least for Momma, was not the same as working in a garden. Instead of feeling satisfied, all she felt was tired.

"This is so hard." Her elbows were on the table, and her face was hidden in her hands.

"It will get easier."

"I don't know how much longer I can do this."

"Not much longer, Momma. I'm thinking of a plan."

She looked up at me. "Oh, Pet. When you say things like that, it makes me want to slap and hug you at the same time."

I was silent. Her mascara was smudged into black rings under her eyes, and her hair had come loose from her long ponytail. She looked so worn out, like if she were my child instead of my momma, I'd take her by the hand and lead her to her room and sit by her side, humming till she fell asleep.

"You should go to bed, Momma."

She nodded. "Right as usual. Maybe you should be the mother, huh? You sure couldn't do a worse job than I am." She wiped her eyes and slowly got up. Before she left, she put a hand on top of my head. "I love you, Pet."

"I know, Momma," I said. "Don't worry."

She went into the living room and lay down on the couch. She and Daddy didn't sleep in the same room anymore. I stayed where I was, in the kitchen, till she fell asleep.

Then I got up and went into Daddy's room. He'd left the curtain open, so moonlight flooded through the window, giving the room a dreamlike glow.

He was on his back, still as a statue, the wrapping paper from Simon's metal detector still scattered across the mattress. On top of his chest lay the instructions. In the light of the moon, I could make out the heading at the top: *Important! Save me!*

I went over to the bed and gently touched his hurt arm. He didn't stir. "You are important," I said, "and I will save you."

I thought of Momma, so tired that she cried herself to sleep at night. I thought of poor Simon, who could only say a single word. I thought of that brown, barren rectangle in the backyard.

"I will save all of you," I whispered, and the instant I said it, my mind began to hum.

Now I knew exactly what to do.

Chapter 8

I **set my alarm for three a.m. The sisters said** their first prayers of the day at three-thirty, so that would give me plenty of time. I put on a jacket and snuck by Momma, who was still asleep on the couch. I stepped out into the boundless night.

Because I'm being one hundred percent truthful, I will tell you: It was a little scary, walking alone down the road in the middle of the night. I heard sounds that sent shivers to my bones: footsteps, cracking branches, a low, low moan.

This is good practice, I thought, *for later.*

I kept on walking till I came to the *Our Lady of Perpetual Help Abbey* sign, which was illuminated by the moonlight.

I had never visited the chapel at this time of day, but I found my way to the heavy doors. Inside, a single candle burned on the stone altar, and the space was completely silent. I took a seat in the front pew.

A bell rang. The nuns filed in, looking spectral in their white robes. They took their places and immediately began to sing. There was a flute whose notes sounded like running water. The whole thing was so soft and ethereal, with the candle burning, all blurry and bright, that I must have fallen asleep. The next thing I knew, the sisters were filing back out of the chapel.

I stood up. Had she not seen me? It was so dark, maybe—

A fluttering white ghost drifted quickly across the chapel and stopped at the gate.

"What are you doing here, Perpetua? Is something wrong?" Sister Melanie whispered, her glasses reflecting the candle's glow.

I was so happy to see her that my words came out all in a jumble. "I thought you didn't see me. Everything's fine. I've got it all figured out. Tell me about the monk, please. Is what Mrs. Minnow said true?"

"Slow down," Sister Melanie whispered. "Who is Mrs. Minnow?"

"She's my neighbor." I forced myself to take a deep

breath and start at the beginning. "She said a monk hid a valuable coin at the abbey. Is that true?"

"I'm familiar with the rumor." Sister Melanie spoke slowly. "But I don't know if it's true."

"Tell me what you know. *Please,*" I added quickly, because I didn't want to sound bossy.

Sister Melanie hesitated. "Perpetua, you aren't going to try to find it, are you?"

"I might."

She was silent, as if trying to figure something out. Then, after a long time, she said, "His name was Brother Brendan. He came to Iowa from Ireland one hundred and fifty years ago, during the great potato famine, in hopes of establishing a monastery. An Irish benefactor, a rich and powerful merchant, gave him a case of gold coins to sell, here in the New World, in order to secure the needed land. One of the coins was especially valuable, at least from a spiritual perspective. It was said to be the very coin that Christ himself held when the Pharisees asked whether they should pay their taxes to Caesar.

"Brother Brendan came by boat with a group of monks, one of whom was a young novice named Jesper. It became obvious to Brendan almost immediately that Jesper would not stay long with the community. The young man was selfish and egotistical and expressed an unseemly interest in the coins.

"Jesper asked about the coins daily and seemed obsessed with trying to calculate their value. Brother Brendan even found a list the young man had made on a bit of brown paper, detailing all the things he would buy—if he could sell the coins.

"Brendan began to guard the coins with his life, keeping them on his person at all times. When the monks finally arrived in Iowa, he quickly secured two hundred acres from a farmer: the very land you and I now stand on. Brendan gave the farmer all the coins in exchange for the acreage, save one: the Christ coin, which he thought far too valuable to trade.

"Knowing Jesper would steal the coin should he ever become aware of its existence inside the monastery, Brendan decided to hide it somewhere *outside* the cloister. He intended to retrieve the coin as soon as Jesper left the order, and then put it on public display in the chapel.

"Jesper did end up deserting the monks a few

months later, still seething over the sold coins. Brother Brendan, however, had suddenly become very ill. Lying immobile in bed, he tried to tell his brother monks where he had hidden the coin. But his mind was foggy, his voice weak. No one could understand what he said.

"Search parties were formed. The monks themselves looked, of course. Then they reached out to local farmers. Word spread, and soon people traveled from all over to search. This went on for years, decades. The last of the monks died, the monastery closed, and then my sisters took over the property and built the abbey. But still, to this day, the coin has never been found."

"The coin—it would be enough to pay for a surgery, right?" I asked.

"Many, many surgeries," Sister Melanie said.

"Good. I think I can find it."

"Oh, Perpetua." She shook her head. "You and thousands of others."

"Actually, I *know* I can find it."

Sister Melanie bit her lip. "You are a child, and I have no intention of blemishing your innocence, but I must tell you that there are bad people in this world. And not a few of them have tried to find the coin.

Someone might be out there right now, hunting for it, even as we speak."

"I know there are bad people," I said, and instantly thought of Mrs. Minnow's son, Gordon, and his angry amber eyes. How he had threatened to break me, like the eggs. "I have to be tough and brave."

"Brave, Perpetua, but not foolish."

"I promised I would save Daddy. I don't believe in breaking promises. Do you?" I stared at her.

"Let's pray for your father," Sister Melanie almost pleaded.

I shook my head. "I tried praying. Now I'm going to try something else."

At that moment, the candle on the altar went out. The chapel was bathed in darkness.

Sister Melanie gasped. "Oh, Perpetua. This isn't a good sign."

I could no longer make out her face. "Maybe. But maybe not. Isn't it always darkest before the light?"

She grabbed me and hugged me across the metal gate. "You silly, headstrong girl."

I smiled. This is why I had come. I needed her blessing.

"Do you have your saltshaker?"

"It's in my pocket," I told her.

"Keep it there." She pulled away. "I have to go. Please be careful, Perpetua."

"I will."

"Don't give up."

"I won't. *Aut viam inveniam aut faciem.*"

I shall either find a way or make one.

Chapter 9

When I got back from the abbey, it was only a couple of hours till Momma would wake. I had to hurry. There was so much to do. As I worked, I recited Mrs. Minnow's poem, over and over, under my breath:

> *"Harden not your heart*
> *That is the place to start*
> *Enchantment is advancement*
> *Fear will draw you near*
> *Though the cave be dark and dreary*
> *Little ones won't grow weary*
> *When upon the rock they find*
> *The coin that leads to peace of mind"*

First, I filled our backpacks. Simon's was a little kid's size, so it couldn't hold much. Truthfully, it would have been easier to leave Simon at home. He would only slow me down and make things more difficult. But I couldn't leave him. Who would take care of him, with Momma working all the time and Daddy in such a sorry state? No, he had to come with me.

I snuck into his room, opened his dresser, and pulled out a change of clothes and a sweatshirt. Back in my room, I packed the same for myself. Then, like a thief, I snuck through the house, gathering supplies: flashlight, matches, rope, scissors, Band-Aids, hammer. I filled two of Daddy's big water bottles. I found an extra blanket.

Food was tricky. One, I had no idea how long we'd be gone. Two, any food we took we had to carry. Three, it had to be nonperishable. And four, our cupboards were kind of bare. When you don't have a lot of money, you don't have a lot of food, either. I thought I could get by on one meal a day, but Simon would need breakfast, lunch, and dinner.

I stood surveying my choices. A loaf of bread was out of the question. It would just get squashed. Cheese had to be refrigerated. Stew would require pots and spoons, which I didn't have room to take. Finally, I decided on crackers, peanut butter, pepperoni, and a pouch of tuna. I dumped it all into our backpacks.

Next, I needed to write a letter so Momma and Daddy wouldn't think Simon and I had been kidnapped. I had to let them know we were okay, but I couldn't tell them too much, in case they tried to stop me.

This is what I came up with:

Dear Momma and Daddy,

I love you both so much. I wanted to say that right off the bat so you didn't think I had run away. Don't worry. I haven't been kidnapped, either.

I made a promise, Momma, if you remember, the other night in the kitchen. It's the same promise I made to you, Daddy, when you were asleep in your bed. I said I would fix everything, as soon as I figured out how. Well, here's some good news: I figured it out. I know how to get the money to pay for Daddy's surgery. And I know how to make it so that you won't have to work such long shifts at Carlton's, Momma. That's why I left.

Simon is with me. I will take very good care of him. I brought food, water, and a blanket.

You are probably nervous, reading this. I know how scared grown-ups get. Please don't be scared. I am tough and brave. I will be okay. Simon will be okay. We will all be okay.

I can't wait to show you what I find!

Yours truly, responsibly, devotedly,
Perpetua

I placed the letter under my pillow for safekeeping.

Then I brewed a pot of coffee for Momma and fried her an egg because this was how I wanted her to remember me, later. After she had found the letter, I wanted her to think of me making breakfast. In control.

I heard her get up and shuffle to the bathroom. The shower turned on. I heard her blow-dry her hair. Then she came into the kitchen with fresh mascara and a tight, new ponytail. She saw the mug and plate I'd set out for her.

"What are you doing up so early, Pet?"

"Making you breakfast," I said, pulling out her chair.

"Oh, honey. I don't have time for breakfast." Momma was always nicest in the morning, when she was still a little foggy with sleep.

"Sure you do. Look. It's all made."

She smiled sort of sadly and sat down. "An eleven-year-old girl shouldn't have to make her mother breakfast."

"I didn't have to. I wanted to," I said, and took the seat across from her.

I watched her eat her egg and sip her coffee. We didn't talk about anything worrying. We didn't talk at all. It was almost like old times, nice and peaceful, side by side in the garden. I could see how Daddy, looking out his window, could pretend he was in a different world.

"I have to go, Pet," Momma said. She reached across the table and touched my hand. "Thank you."

I felt a little bit guilty. She was acting so friendly, not knowing that when she got off work this evening both of her children would be gone.

I handed her her purse and waved goodbye from the screen door as she backed the car onto the road. "Forgive me, Momma, for deceiving you," I said, and stood there, watching, until I couldn't see the car anymore.

After Momma left, I made oatmeal for Simon and me. While I waited for him to wake up, I packed our lunches: bologna sandwiches and carrot sticks. I was putting away the mayonnaise when there was a knock at the kitchen door.

It was Mrs. Minnow, her hair fiery red in the morning sun.

"Oh dear," she said. "I'm sorry to bother you so early, but I wanted to give you this." She handed me two baggies of vanilla wafer cookies. "In case you get hungry, you know." She seemed more agitated than usual, so I tried to soothe her.

"Thank you so much. These will be the perfect snack."

She grabbed my wrist. Her fingernails were painted blue. "Gordon's looking for it," she stammered. "He started as soon as the sun came up. Oh dear."

I was not surprised, or afraid, or concerned. I knew Gordon would hunt for the coin. I also knew—at least, I was pretty sure I knew—he wouldn't find it.

"He has weapons." Mrs. Minnow's hands were doing their birdlike fluttering.

"What kind?" I wondered. Daddy's the one who taught me to size up an enemy. It's important before you face off to know exactly what you're up against.

"Knives. Traps. Oh dear."

How I would've liked to help her not worry so much, but my plate was so full of helping that I couldn't right then. Mrs. Minnow would have to fix her own problems. "Thank you for the warning," I told her. "And the cookies."

"Oh dear" was all she could say before hurrying off down the road.

I decided to wake up Simon. Usually, Cookie Boy was up bright and early. It just figured that the one day I needed him to rise with the roosters was the day he decided to play Sleeping Beauty.

"Simon," I said, pulling down his dinosaur sheet. "Wake up. It's time to have an adventure."

Simon sat up and immediately replaced his crown, which had fallen off in the night. "Cheese?" he said, which meant, "Where's Momma?" He asked the same exact thing every morning.

"She's at the restaurant," I told him. I set him out a T-shirt and shorts. As he changed, I tried to explain the plan. "We have a mission. We have to save Momma and Daddy. You want to save them, don't you?"

Simon nodded. I led him to the bathroom and combed his hair. Then I helped him brush his teeth, which was about as much fun as trying to paint a cat's claws. You'd think I was poking around in his mouth with a screwdriver, the way he was fussing. So much did I hate dealing with Simon's squirming that I thought about leaving our toothbrushes behind. But I knew Momma would be disappointed if we came home with cavities, even if we were carrying a lost coin of the Ancient World. So I added toothbrushes to our backpacks, even though I didn't want to.

As we ate our oatmeal, I realized I was like a general, and my brother was a soldier whom I was leading into battle. So I needed to give a rousing speech that would make him commit to my plan. I thought for a minute. Then, this is what I told him: "Life is like a game, Simon. It's like Candy Land. You start out at the beginning, just a baby, and you've got to get to the candy house at the end."

Simon shoveled a big brown-sugary bite of oatmeal into his mouth.

"What do you think the candy house represents?" I asked.

"Cheese," he said.

"That's right: happiness. Now, sometimes on the way to the house, you draw a good card—say, the ice cream floats. And then you're so close to happiness, you can almost taste the candy in your mouth. But sometimes you're going along, and you've gotten really far, and then you land in the Molasses Swamp."

"Cheese," Simon sighed.

"Exactly. You're stuck in the swamp, and there's no way to get to the candy house till you draw the right card. And that's exactly what's happened to us, Simon. Daddy landed in the swamp, and now we're all stuck."

My brother nodded and used his spoon to dig a swampy hole in the middle of his oatmeal.

"That's the bad news," I continued. "The good news is this: I know how to get to the candy house. I know where the card is hidden that will get us out of this swamp."

"Cheese?" Simon said hopefully.

"Well, I don't know the *exact* spot where it's hidden," I admitted. I didn't want him to think our mission would be *too* easy. "But I know what the card looks like—it's an old silver coin—and I know its general location: somewhere on the two hundred acres of the abbey. Do you want to help me find it?"

Simon dipped his finger into a pool of melted butter, then licked it. "Cheese," he said.

Which I knew meant, "Yes."

The final thing to decide before we left was whether to say goodbye to Daddy. I wanted to see him, of course, but I was afraid Simon, once he was with Daddy, wouldn't want to leave him. Sometimes, in the morning especially, Simon would snuggle up beside him in bed, and the two of them would stare out the window for hours, silent as stones.

In the end, though, I chose to see him because I could not bear the thought of *not* seeing him one last time.

I knocked on his door. "Would you like some breakfast, Daddy?"

"Not today," he said, which was what he said every day. But then he said, "I need to ask you something." Which he had never said before.

I opened the door. There my daddy was, sitting in bed in a white T-shirt. Simon did a running jump and wormed his way under Daddy's good arm.

"What were you doing out there?" Daddy asked me. His voice sounded strange, sort of like he was in awe.

"Um, eating oatmeal," I said, a little confused because there is nothing awe-inspiring about a bowl of warm oats.

"Outside, I mean," Daddy said. "What were you doing outside?"

Now I was very confused. "We weren't outside."

"Yes, you were. I saw you. You were wearing your crown." He glanced down at Simon. "You had a scepter in your hand and were riding a little white pony. And you, Pet." Here he turned to me. "You were guiding the horse by its reins. The wind blew, and your hair was a flag behind you. And the look on your face—it was so determined. The sun was shining, and you were all illuminated. It's like I was looking at a painting in a museum."

"I think you had a vision, Daddy," I said. Sister Melanie had told me about visions.

But Daddy didn't hear me. "A painting," he said again. "A real-life painting." He sounded a little out of breath.

"I sure do love you," I told him, and coaxed Simon out from under his arm. "See you later, Daddy."

We stepped into the hallway.

It was time. Time to make Daddy's vision a reality. Time to steal a pony.

Chapter 10

Our backpacks were stuffed. We'd eaten our breakfast, said our goodbyes. I'd placed the letter where I knew Momma would find it: on top of her pillow, which was still on the couch from last night. We were just putting on our shoes when Simon said, "Cheese, cheese," and ran from the kitchen. He came back carrying his scepter in one hand and the metal detector in the other. The box of taffies was tucked under his arm.

Now, I was pleased he wanted to bring along the scepter, since I'd made it for him, and there was no denying that a metal detector might come in handy, looking for a lost coin. But I didn't know how to bring them with us. It seemed unwise to have our hands completely full. "Simon, we're going to have to leave those behind."

He stuck out his lip, and a big, fat tear slipped out of one eye. He looked like the saddest Cookie Boy in the world.

"Maybe I can figure something out," I relented. I took a piece of rope from the backpack and used it to strap the scepter and metal detector crosswise across his back. "There. What do you think of that?"

He put his hands on his hips and nodded approvingly.

"Good. So here's the deal: We have to leave the taffies behind. There's no room in our backpacks. But I'll give you one now." I took a taffy from the box, unwrapped it, and popped it in his mouth. "And I promise that as soon as we get home, you can eat the rest, all in one sitting. Deal?"

Simon nodded.

"Then let's go."

It was warm and windy as Simon and I made our way down the road to Holly's. One thing I hadn't considered was that strapping the scepter and metal detector to Simon's small frame would leave no space for his backpack. Which meant I had to carry two: mine on my back and his small one on my front. I felt like a mix between a turtle and a potbellied bear.

Just to be clear: I did not want to take a pony from our grouchy neighbor. It was not my goal in life to be a horse thief. But I knew there was no way Simon could make the journey on foot. Already he was stubbing the toes of his sneakers.

And I probably should speak more precisely. I wasn't *stealing* Crystal. I was *borrowing* her. As soon as we found the coin, I would give her back.

You might wonder how I intended to steal a pony out from under Holly's nose in broad daylight. Well, I hadn't figured that out yet.

We stopped when we got to his ramshackle house, dawdling by the mailbox while I tried to decide what to do. Just then the dented screen door burst open and out stepped grumpy old Holly himself.

He made a shooing motion as we came toward him. "No time. Go away," he grumbled.

"Mr. Hollis—" I began.

"Ya got corncobs in your ears?" he interrupted. "No time. Go away." He headed toward the driveway.

"We were just wondering—"

"How big of a pest you could be?" He opened the door of his rusted pickup truck. "I've got a list of errands a mile long. No time to chat with you knuckle-heads. Go away."

"We will, sir," I said, "but would you mind if we

visited the ponies before we left?" See, if he gave us permission to visit, it wouldn't be stealing. For all I knew, the technical definition of *visiting* might include taking an animal on a coin-hunting expedition. I didn't happen to have a dictionary in my backpack, so it was impossible to know for sure.

Holly looked at me, then at Simon, his face the usual grimace. "Why's he still wearing that ugly crown?"

"He likes it," I said firmly.

"Huh," Holly grunted. "Takes all kinds." He got into his truck and started the engine. Then he rolled down the window and hollered, "Yeah, you can visit 'em. Just don't let 'em loose."

"We won't," I said, and that was the truth. Crystal would not be loose. I'd hold her by the reins the entire time.

In the barn, we went straight to her stall and found her standing perfectly still in its center. Her white coat glowed and her blond mane shone as she stared at us with her clear blue eyes.

"Good morning," I said. "We need your help."

I removed my backpacks slowly so as not to startle her. Then I stepped into her stall and ran my hand down her smooth forelock. I helped Simon do the same.

I'd watched Holly prep her so many times that I was confident I could do it myself. All of her supplies

hung from hooks along the wall. I slid the bridle onto her head, placed the heavy saddle on her back. She remained perfectly still. "Good girl," I murmured, and offered her a couple of sugar cubes from Holly's stash on the shelf.

Then I helped Simon climb on top of her. What a sight he was, perched on that pony, a grin as wide as the Mississippi spread across his Cookie Boy face.

"Cheese!" he cried triumphantly.

I put on the backpacks and led Crystal out of the barn, my heart skipping a beat at the possibility of Holly changing his mind about running errands. But the driveway was empty. No truck. No grouch.

Taking that pony turned out to be as easy as taking a blind dog's bone.

Down the road the three of us went, a strange sight, I'm sure, had anyone been around to see us. As we walked, I thought of the coin. So certain was I of finding it that I could almost feel its weight in my palm.

We reached the abbey sign. It was only then that I realized I might not have thought everything about this adventure through. For example: How would I, wearing two backpacks and leading a pony carrying a five-year-old king, sneak past the nuns?

I wasn't wearing a watch (my battery had died, and Momma said there was not one single cent to replace it), so I wasn't sure of the time. But no matter what the sisters were doing at this particular moment—praying in the chapel, making taffies in the factory—all one of them would have to do is glance out the window. And then Simon and I would have some explaining to do. Even worse, what if they were down at the henhouse, and here comes Crystal clip-clopping past? To think my whole plan could vanish like a tooth left under a pillow—it made me shiver under the midsummer sun.

Nevertheless, I continued.

Fortes fortuna juvat.

Fortune aids the brave.

We made our way past the candy factory. No one tried to stop us. We came in view of the chapel. Not a single white robe appeared. Down the steep road to the farmhouse. Not a sister in sight.

What we did see were the chickens, strutting about in the henhouse yard, searching for bugs for breakfast. They looked up when we approached, and the three black-and-white-spotted Barred Rocks broke off from the group, pecking their way to the road. Soon, Faith, Hope, and Charity had situated themselves in the middle of our path.

"Sorry, girls, but there's no time for visiting today," I called. "You're going to have to get out of the way."

Faith and Charity heeded my words and strutted back over to the grass. But Hope, Simon's little egg-less favorite, flapped her wings and settled herself down atop an invisible pavement nest.

I had to stop our caravan.

As soon as I did, Simon slid off Crystal's back and raced to his beloved bird. He scooped her up and buried his face in her feathers.

"We don't have time for this, Simon," I said.

My brother tucked Hope under one arm, then stuck a shoe in the saddle's stirrup and pulled himself up onto Crystal's back.

"Cheese," he said, which I think meant, "You may continue."

I was quite certain Daddy's vision did not include

a chicken. But then again, Hope was small, so maybe she was nestled in Simon's lap all along and Daddy just couldn't see her.

"Giddyap, Crystal." I gave the reins a gentle tug.

Off we started, not knowing who was watching us.

Chapter 11

I led Crystal, who carried Simon and Hope, down a gravel road that cut across a wide valley. The valley was beautiful, lush and green, part field, part forest, rolling, then climbing in all directions.

It was maybe ten o'clock in the morning, I guessed. Daddy could tell time just by looking at the sun, and now I wished I'd asked him to teach me. Simon, though, didn't bother trying to parse the heavens for clues. He just listened to the rumble of his belly. Right now, his belly was rumbling, *Feed me*.

"Cheese?" he called.

This was one of the few times when cheese actually meant cheese.

"It's too early to eat, Cookie Boy. We can't go

through all our food in the first two hours." I didn't glance back at him, but I knew his face was pinched into a knot of unhappiness.

We trudged on. As the sun rose higher, the air grew hotter. I cuffed the sleeves of my T-shirt and put my hair in a ponytail.

I didn't have a map of the nuns' property. This was a problem, I realized. I had no way of knowing which parts were woods, which parts had been cleared for cattle. The green hills undulated in every direction. It was impossible to see where they ended.

I will admit that I felt my first doubt, then. It made my insides hollow and my head foggy. A part of me wanted to turn back, go tell Momma my ridiculous plan. "Oh, Pet," she'd say. "What were you thinking? No way a child's going to find a coin that adults haven't been able to for decades. And even if you did, those nuns would probably keep it."

Now, my momma didn't really say that, mind you. Those words were what I *imagined* she'd say. Nevertheless, they added a whole other layer of trouble. See, I'd never considered this basic fact: The coin was on the nuns' land, which meant it belonged to them. The momma of my mind was right: If I found it, they might not let me keep it.

I wondered, in that moment, if I felt how Daddy

must have felt: like no matter what you did or tried, it wouldn't be enough, so there was no sense in doing or trying anymore. Or maybe I was like Momma, who wouldn't plant seeds because spring was a season she no longer believed in.

Simon whimpered. He was still hungry. Crystal stopped in her tracks. She was tired of walking. And oh dear, as Mrs. Minnow would say, I thought of another thing I hadn't planned for: water. Crystal could eat grass, but she would need something to drink. I would have to find a creek. Somehow.

It was officially hot now, and I was sweating. Maybe there were some tears mixed in with the sweat, too. I could feel defeat and that hardening that starts to happen inside you, so that you can still stand up under the weight of disappointment.

I thought of my daddy again, the way he'd almost fossilized in that bed. I thought of Momma's empty garden.

And then I thought of the poem:

Harden not your heart
That is the place to start
Enchantment is advancement
Fear will draw you near
Though the cave be dark and dreary

Little ones won't grow weary
When upon the rock they find
The coin that leads to peace of mind

I realized something then. I had a choice. That's what Sister Melanie said. "Each day you choose, Perpetua, how you will live in the world. Happy or sad. Loving or hateful. Timid or brave. Your life is a choice, every single day."

Oh, Momma had not liked that when I told her. "You think I chose this?" she said late one night after twelve hours at the restaurant. "You think your father chose this?"

No, I didn't think my parents had chosen their misfortune. And yet, there was something in Sister Melanie's words that rang true.

I had a choice, right now, sweating in this valley. I could believe, or I could doubt. I could hope, or I could despair. I could be brave or full of fear. I could give up, or I could anticipate the change of seasons.

I'd already chosen on previous occasions to be brave and believe in a future that was better than the present. What I realized now, though, was that choosing once or twice wasn't enough. I had to choose the better part over and over again. As Sister Melanie said, "Every single day."

So I did. I chose for Momma, who didn't know she got to choose; for Daddy, who had made the wrong choice; and for Simon, who didn't know what choosing was.

"I am not afraid! I won't give up!" I let my words ring through the green valley. Then I turned to Simon and said, "Let's search here."

I led Crystal to the shade of an oak tree and helped Simon down from her back. Hope flapped her wings, hopped from his arms, and began to scour the ground for insects. I untied the scepter and metal detector from Simon's chubby body. He took the gifts I'd made him and ran through the field, jumping and leaping like a snake-bitten cat. I slowly waved Nana's present across the grass.

It was while using the metal detector that I first got the feeling. It started as a prick in my neck, then the goose bumps spread all down my arms and back.

Someone was watching me.

Valley spread before me, and to my right was cattle fencing. But to my left were woods so thick that I could barely see past the first line of trees.

I paused and stared. I heard the

call of a great horned owl and the rustle of leaves in a sudden gust of wind. I couldn't see anything, but I knew someone was there. *Someone,* not something. A chill ran down my spine.

"Come on, Simon," I called. "Let's get out of here."

He came running obediently toward me. I lifted him onto Crystal's saddle and handed him the chicken.

"I'm sorry, girl," I told the pony. "I know that wasn't much of a rest. Next time, I promise, will be longer."

She tossed her head like she didn't believe me.

We moved on. Every few minutes, I'd glance behind us, but no one was there. No one I could see, that is. *Somebody* was there, following, invisible, from a distance. The goose bumps told me so. They were a warning siren on my skin.

You might think me foolish, but I didn't realize how big two hundred acres was till I was in the midst of it. Now that I was standing there, wearing double backpacks, the leader of a little caravan, it struck me that trying to find a coin in this amount of land was like trying to find a missing earring in a shopping mall. I didn't know where to begin. I was looking for a cave, I supposed, but a cave was nowhere on the horizon. And what if *cave* in the poem didn't really mean *cave*? What if *cave* was code for something else, like a creek or a grove of trees?

I was a bit overwhelmed, but I didn't despair.

I'd already made my choice for the day.

The sun was straight overhead, which I figured meant noon, time for lunch. We came to a circle of pine trees, and that seemed the perfect fairy-tale spot to sit and eat, spread out upon a bed of green needles.

Inside the pine ring, Simon ran laps as I dug our lunches from the backpack. We ate our bologna sandwiches side by side, in the center of the shady circle. I gave Crystal my carrots as an apology for that first short rest. She crunched them lazily, her eyes half open. For dessert there were Mrs. Minnow's vanilla cookies. I smashed one of my own and let Hope peck the sweet crumbs from my hand.

It felt safe inside the ring of pines, like we were protected by fortress walls. I forgot about the eyes that had spent the morning crawling across my back. My goose bumps faded, and I thought about Brother Brendan, the monk who'd hidden the coin. I tried to imagine, if I were he, where I would have placed it. In a hollow stump? A groundhog's hole? The possibilities were endless, but the poem was quite clear:

> *Though the cave be dark and dreary*
> *Little ones won't grow weary*

There was a cave. There had to be a cave.

And yet, I hadn't seen a single rock formation. It was a mystery.

"A beautiful mystery," Sister Melanie would say. That's what she called things that were beyond comprehension, and she'd smile, fully content, when she said it.

I wasn't sure I agreed with her, though. Mysteries might be beautiful, but they were meant to be solved.

I turned to Simon, who was sitting cross-legged, nibbling his cookies, scepter and metal detector laid out beside him. "What would you buy with the money? After Daddy's surgery was paid for," I quickly added.

Simon took a drink from his water bottle, closed his eyes, and swished the liquid around in his mouth. "Cheese," he said at last.

"Does that mean an electric train set?"
He nodded.

"Well, I'll tell you what I would buy," I said, even though I was on the verge of sounding greedy. But it is very hard when imagining finding a valuable coin not to imagine what you would buy with it. "Some walkie-talkies. A ukulele. A watch with a solar battery." I paused. "But first I'd buy Momma a stainless-steel watering can, and Holly two new ponies to replace the ones that died. And I'd buy Mrs. Minnow a new front door, with five dead bolts, so she could lock that mean ol' son of hers out of the house."

Simon laughed so hard that water sprayed from his mouth.

And that's when I heard it, when it was too late. The sound of foot-steps. Harsh, ragged breaths.

"Who you calling mean?" an angry voice said.

Chapter 12

Gordon stood behind us, dressed in a T-shirt and camouflage pants, his gray hair looking scraggier than ever. Maybe it was a trick of the shadows, but he seemed bigger than he did inside Mrs. Minnow's house. His arms were stretched tight with muscles. And the expression on his face was even colder, even harder. *Sinister* was the word that slithered through my head.

All of us—Crystal, Hope, Simon, and I—froze at the sight of him. Upon first hearing his voice, I had jumped up and gripped Simon's hand, but now we stood as still as statues.

"Ain't so funny now, is it?" Gordon snarled.

Simon whimpered. I squeezed his hand.

Gordon smiled. He was made happy by our fear, the way a wolf gets excited by an injured lamb. He glanced at our little menagerie, and his smile grew bigger.

"Well, ain't you a couple of real-life explorers. Got you a horse and everything. Too bad she ain't bigger, or I could use her."

Crystal flared her nostrils and stamped a hoof into the pine needles.

"I think she likes me," Gordon said. He lifted a hunk of her mane. "Pretty hair. I bet somebody'd pay good money for that."

"Don't touch her," I said. I tried to make my voice sound tough, but it came out thin and fragile.

Gordon spit on the ground and ignored me. "Yeah, real pretty." He put a hand on her tail. Then his eyes fell on Hope. "Mmm. I didn't know you had a chicken. I like chicken."

Quick as a canine, he lunged at the bird. Next thing I knew, Gordon was holding Hope upside down by the legs. She beat her wings madly, trying to escape, but the only thing she loosed was a handful of feathers, which drifted like dandelion seeds to the ground.

"Cheese!" Simon screamed. Before I could stop him, he broke free from my grasp and went running toward Gordon, arms swinging, like something feral.

Oh, that Cookie Boy was on fire, all for the love of a bird. He kicked and smacked and screamed till Gordon lost his grip, and Hope made a beeline for the deeper woods. I don't know if you've ever seen a chicken run, but they can put a cheetah to shame, let me tell you.

Gordon was furious. The veins in his neck bulged, and his eyes glared. "I thought I told you to keep away from my treasure," he snarled.

"The treasure doesn't belong to you," I said. Maybe Simon's rage was an inspiration, because my voice sounded a little stronger—even though my heart was beating so fast it felt like my body might shake into a million pieces.

Gordon got so close to me then that I could see the whiskers on his chin. He pointed a crooked finger in my face. "That, little girl, is where you're wrong. See, if I find the coin, it's mine. And if you find the coin . . ." He flashed a sharp-toothed grin. "Well, let's just say I know how to make sure it's mine then, too."

Maybe I was too scared to say anything in reply. Or maybe I was too wise. "You beware of Gordon," Momma had told me. I was being ware. I was biting my tongue but honing my eyes.

Gordon spit on the ground again.

Then he saw the metal detector.

"Well, I'll be." He walked over to where it was lying beside Simon's scepter. "Where'd you get this?"

"Nana," I said without thinking.

"*Nana,*" he said mockingly. He picked up the detector and waved it foolishly in the air. "Don't work."

"You have to turn it on," I told him.

Gordon looked at me slyly out of the corner of his eye, that wicked smile tickling his lips. "Show me."

Maybe you've heard of win-win situations, where no matter what choice you make, everything comes out fine and dandy. Well, this was not one of those times. This was what I call a lose-lose situation. Lose-lose is when you have to make a decision even though there are no *good* decisions left. If I showed him, he'd know how to work the thing. But if I didn't show him, I was certain one of us—Simon, Crystal, Hope, or me—would end up hurt.

I took the metal detector and pushed the big red ON button. "There," I said, and demonstrated how to wave it in a more sensible manner.

"Ha ha," Gordon cackled, and grabbed it from my hands. "Thanks for the new toy."

You can be assured I knew that was going to happen. If a bad guy gets a chance to rob you, he'll take it. But I'll tell you something else. I didn't care that he had the metal detector. Somehow, I knew the coin would not be found using it.

What I did care about was him having Simon's gift. It's a pretty rotten thing to steal a birthday present from a five-year-old. Sure, Momma was just going to sell it. But your momma selling a toy to pay the bills is in a whole different boat than a criminal stealing it right from under your nose.

Now, normally, I don't have too much of a temper. Momma says I'm cool as Jack Frost from head to toe. But the longer I looked at mean ol' Gordon, readying to take off with Simon's gift, the angrier I got. Sister Melanie says too much anger can rob a person's reason. I never knew what she meant by that, but I was about to find out.

"Give it back, you big bully!" I screamed, and then I leaned forward like a football player and made a hard dash for his chest.

I hit him square in the ribs. Gordon skidded backward, then fell to the ground, dropping the metal detector in the process. He lay on his back for several seconds, unmoving. I think he was in shock.

Simon ran forward and scooped his present off the ground.

That broke Gordon's stupor. "You little—" he snarled, and was up on his feet before I could blink.

Simon grabbed hold of Crystal's saddle with one hand, like a cowboy, and swung himself onto her back.

"Give me that," Gordon said. He grasped the detector and pulled, trying to wrench it from Simon's grip.

It all happened so quickly. Before I could think. Before I could act.

Gordon, still trying to pry away the detector, grabbed hold of Simon's shoulder.

That's when my brother bit.

Oh, it was a good bite, too. I heard the crunch of tooth against finger. Gordon yanked his hand away and howled.

"Cheese," Simon whispered, which either meant "Sorry" or "If you touch me again, I'll bite off your whole hand."

Gordon was in no mood for either interpretation.

"You wanna fight? Let's fight." With a mighty yank, he ripped the metal detector from Simon's hands.

Things slowed down then, just like they did when Daddy fell. I saw Simon's mouth form an *O* of anguish. I saw his body slip from the saddle, then float, head-first, to the ground.

"*Aaahhh,*" Simon cried, one long, slow note.

Gordon lifted his right knee, then his left. As if in quicksand, he ran.

Slowly, so slowly, I made my way to Simon, to where he lay with his face pressed into the ground. I turned him over. That's when time sped up again.

When I saw my baby brother covered in blood, his body spread out on a bed of pine needles.

Chapter 13

I screamed. **Simon screamed. Our voices min-** gled together, one horrible, high-pitched wail. Then I stopped screaming. I chose to stop. And so choosing, I helped Simon choose to stop, too.

Blood was everywhere. It was smeared across his cheeks, neck, the front of his shirt.

"Oh, Simon, where's it coming from?" Frantically, I searched his body for the wound.

"Cheese," he mumbled. His teeth were red.

Finally, I found it. He had a deep cut on his mouth. Part of his top lip had been severed and now hung like a flap. I tore through my backpack till I found my extra T-shirt. I balled it up and pressed it to his wound.

Simon whimpered as tears slid from his eyes.

"Cookie Boy, I'm so sorry this happened to you," I said. And then I started crying, too. My tears fell on his face and made little riverbeds in the blood.

Crystal came over, snorted, and shook her head. I was just thinking that we'd probably never see Hope again, after what Gordon had done to her, when her black-and-white head poked out from behind a nearby pine. Cautiously, she looked this way and that. Coast clear, she strutted over to join us.

I lifted my T-shirt and studied Simon's mouth. The bleeding had stopped, but the dangling lip made me shiver. I had packed Band-Aids, but a Band-Aid couldn't fix this. He needed stitches, which meant we needed to go home.

The coin hunt was over.

"Here. Let's get you up," I said, and gently pulled Simon into a sitting position. "Do you feel dizzy?"

He shook his head, then pointed a chubby finger toward his crown, which had fallen off. I put it back on his head.

"You look like a king who's just fought a terrific battle." I took his hands and tugged him to his feet. Then I helped him onto Crystal's saddle. I scooped up Hope, set her in his lap, and handed him his scepter.

Once my backpacks were on, we were ready. "Giddyap," I said.

Crystal was as obedient as ever.

There was only one problem, but it was a big one. I didn't know how to get home.

What I'm about to tell you will make me seem incredibly foolish. When I was planning our adventure and imagining that coin in my palm, I never thought about *after*. What I mean is, I pictured us wandering for days, wading through streams, trekking across valleys, till at last we found the coin. And that's where my picture ended. I hadn't even considered finding our way back home.

Which meant I'd made no map—not even a mental one—to guide us. Nor had I tied ribbons to branches or scattered bread crumbs to form a trail. No, I'd just walked for hours and hours and gotten us completely, unmistakably lost.

Errare humanum est. To err is human, Sister Melanie always said. And I had erred big-time.

The only thing to do was keep on moving in hopes that by luck or magic we'd somehow end up back at the farmhouse and the winding lane that would lead us home.

We walked for a long time. Hours, I guess. My feet hurt. My body felt like it might crumble under the weight of the backpacks. But my brother's blood pushed me onward. In my letter, I had promised Momma and

Daddy that I would take care of him. And I was a girl who kept her promises.

So we walked—through sun and shade, woods and fields, up hills and down valleys. The sun began its steady slide toward the horizon. Simon was mostly quiet. I made him keep my T-shirt pressed against his mouth. Crystal's pace had slowed considerably. She was tired and thirsty. Time was passing, and yet there was no proof of any progress.

And then I saw it—oh, miracle of miracles—at the bottom of a valley, sparkling and clear as glass. A stream. Water. At that moment, I would have sworn there was nothing more beautiful in the world.

"Look, Simon!" I said. "Look!" I lifted him and Hope from Crystal's back, and as soon as I did, that pony made a mad dash for the stream. Hope followed, frantically weaving her way toward the water.

When Simon and I reached the stream bank, I scrubbed that Cookie Boy clean, washing blood from every fold and surface of his chubby body. I rinsed his bloody shirt in the water, then set it on the bank to dry. Next, I gave Simon his extra shirt to change into.

"Cheese?" he asked once he was looking halfway decent again. (Decent, that is, if you kept your eyes off his mouth.)

"Sure, we can eat supper." I figured it was close

enough to evening, and even if it wasn't, my stomach had turned fierce in its grumbling.

I made us both peanut butter and crackers by spreading out the crackers in the grass. I broke Simon's into tiny baby bites, so scared was I that that hanging lip would be a choking hazard.

Crystal grazed on the lush grass near the stream. Hope clucked by with a worm dangling from her beak. I kept an eye out for Gordon, though I suspected he'd leave us alone now that he had what he thought was our most prized possession.

We had just finished eating when Crystal neighed.

I looked up. There, on the other side of the stream, was a sheep.

"*Baa,*" it said, staring right at me.

Then another sheep joined the first. And another. And another. Soon there was a whole row of sheep, and then a second row, and a third row, and more. There must have been a hundred sheep altogether, wool dusty-white, mouths open in a chorus of bleating.

"Cheese," Simon said, kind of astonished-like.

"I know what you mean," I whispered back.

A figure appeared then and parted the flock with the raising of her hand. Dressed in a purple robe and straw hat, she carried a staff and a leather pack. When she got to the stream bank, I could make out her blond hair and a pale face that was wide and flat.

"Good tidings," she called to us. "Good evening, too."

I put an arm around Simon's shoulders, drawing him close, just as Hope darted over and hopped into his lap. There was something unusual about the woman. She was different from us, I could tell—though I wasn't sure how. I didn't know if she was a friend or an enemy.

"Who are you?" I asked suspiciously.

"I'm Gabby."

And then something happened that I wish I could witness over again, to see if what I think happened really did. Because maybe what I saw, I didn't really see. Maybe it was a trick of the shadows, or something about how her purple robe draped the ground. But I'll tell you what it looked like to me. It looked like the woman, the shepherdess, floated across the stream. And when I say floated, I don't mean swam. I mean her feet didn't touch the water.

She landed in front of us. Her sheep stayed on the other bank, no longer bleating.

"I'm missing one," Gabby said. "A lamb. Looks just like the others. You haven't seen him, by chance?"

"No, ma'am." There was something spooky about her. Her voice was big and loud, but also like a song. Simon shivered beside me.

"You need not be afraid," she sang, reading my mind. "I won't hurt you. Unlike others who lurk in the valley."

I wondered if she meant Gordon, but I didn't ask.

"I can help you," she said.

"We don't need any help," I told her, which I didn't consider a lie since the kind of help we needed—finding our way home, getting Simon to the hospital—I was certain this weird shepherd lady couldn't provide.

Gabby turned her attention to my brother. "You've been injured."

He nodded.

"Does your mouth hurt?"

He nodded again, and this time tears slipped from his dark eyes.

"I can help you," she repeated, and set down her wooden staff. She opened her leather pack and pulled something out, which she then held up between her thumb and forefinger.

It was a spool of thread. But the thread was unlike any I'd ever seen. It was so brilliant white that it glowed.

"I'll stitch his lip," she sang.

All I could do was stare. It was the strangest thing I'd ever heard. It was like something from a dream, one of those ones that even while you're dreaming it you know doesn't make any sense. A flock of sheep, a floating shepherdess, some magic thread.

"He's not going to let you stitch his lip," I told her. That was the most ridiculous part of it. What five-year-old would just sit there while a stranger sewed his lip back on his face? There was no way Simon, who hated to have a comb run through his hair, would allow her to poke a needle through his flesh.

"He'll let me," Gabby said.

I began to doubt her intelligence.

"You want me to fix you?" she asked my brother.

"Cheese," Simon said softly, and though it was hard to believe, I knew "cheese" meant "yes."

"All right. Lie down."

Simon did, right there in the grass. I knelt beside him and held his hand.

Gabby dug through her pack again and pulled out a small glass tube with a golden lid. Its contents glittered silver-like in the fading sun. "Here. We'll just put a little bit of this on. . . ." She crouched low and carefully spread some of the tube's contents on Simon's mouth. "Now you won't feel a thing."

I rolled my eyes, which is rude, but I couldn't help it. I put my mouth to Simon's ear. "Are you sure you want to do this?"

He was silent, eyes closed, silver sparkles on his lips.

Gabby, in the meantime, had found a needle for her glowing thread. She got down on her knees, beside Simon's head.

"*Nunc aut nunquam,*" she said, looking right at me. Now or never.

"I didn't think shepherds knew Latin," I told her.

"Shepherds know a lot of things."

On the other side of the stream, one hundred sheep stood mute, watching. All those yellow eyes were enough to give me the spooky, shivery feeling again.

Gabby raised her needle. Before I could object, she thrust it into my brother's lip.

Chapter 14

He did not cry, believe it or not. In fact, he didn't move at all. He lay there, eyes closed, stock-still, as if he were taking the most restful of naps.

I'd never seen anyone get stitches before—and let me tell you, in case you're wondering, it's not exactly pleasant. It's rather disgusting, actually.

"I could tell you a story," Gabby said, head bent.

"Okay," I told her, not because I wanted to hear a story, but because I thought it might take my mind off the fact that someone was pushing a needle through my brother's flesh.

I was feeling a little queasy, I'm not too proud to admit.

"You know how I like to begin a story?"

"How?" I asked.

"Once upon a time."

How original, I thought.

"Once upon a time," the shepherdess sang, "there was a world, a big, beautiful world. And in this world, there was a family. The family was rich—monetarily, at least. The father was a doctor. The mother was good at investing. They had one child, a daughter, and lived in a grand house filled with many expensive things.

"The daughter was spoiled, of course, as is natural in such circumstances. Anything she wanted, she was given. There were elaborate birthday parties and Christmases with dozens of elegantly wrapped presents. The girl was happy. She loved all her toys, especially a porcelain doll collection that was housed in a glass case in her enormous room.

"But when the girl was ten, tragedy struck. Her father was killed in a car accident. Both mother and daughter were devastated. But they chose to bear their sorrow in different ways. The mother became quite controlling to try to make up for the fact that much of life is beyond our control. She picked out the girl's clothes, did her hair, chose which activities she would participate in. And when the girl was fully grown, she even made a list of acceptable professions and suitors.

"The girl, for her part, gravitated to the opposite

extreme. What was the use in planning, she wondered, when all one's plans could be extinguished in the blink of an eye, or the crash of a car? No, the girl decided, she was through with anything that resembled order. She gave up trying in school—no more memorizing multiplication tables or the parts of plants—and willingly let her mother pack her lunches and pick the music in the car.

"The mother was as bound as a chain. The girl as free as a stringless balloon. Neither was happy. Many years passed. The girl became a woman.

"And here the trouble began.

"You see, she had no interest in her mother's list of professions. She had no interest in any profession at all. She had spent so many years avoiding making choices that she had no idea where to begin.

" 'You have to do something,' the mother said in exasperation.

" 'I am doing something. It's called nothing,' the girl replied.

"The list of suitors was even more poorly received than the list of jobs. The young men whose names the mother had chosen were the epitome of organization: Eagle Scouts and class presidents off to study medicine or law.

"The girl stuck out her tongue when she saw them. 'Yuck.'

" 'Don't be a baby,' said her mother.

"She forced her daughter to go on dates with them, where the daughter acted her rudest. She refused to make eye contact, ignored their compliments, spilled drinks in their laps. By the time the evening was over, none of them wished to see her again.

"Which was exactly what she wanted.

"Then it was summer. A fair came to town. The girl decided to go, out of boredom. She bought cotton candy, played a game where she popped three balloons and won a mirror, rode on a Ferris wheel. And then she saw a boy about her age giving a demonstration. He was carving statues out of wood with a chain saw."

I gasped.

Gabby smiled.

"What happened next?" I asked.

"She fell in love, of course," Gabby said, the needle still between her fingers. "Her mother objected. The boy was poor and uneducated. He was the opposite of everything the mother had planned. Perhaps that's why the girl fell in love.

" 'If you run off with him, you'll be heading to your doom,' the mother warned.

" 'Oh, please,' the girl said.

" 'You want to live as a wild thing? Then live as a wild thing—but I won't support you. Not one dollar, I swear.'

" 'Love is its own reward,' said the girl.

" 'You'll see how rewarding it is to be poor and hungry.'

"Two weeks later, the girl was married.

"What do you think of that?"

It took me a moment to realize Gabby was asking about Simon's lip, not the story. She had finished her stitching.

I knelt over Simon to examine her work. My brother's eyes were sleepy but open, and a hint of a smile tickled the edges of his mouth. As for his lip, it was perfect: no blood, no cut—just the thinnest, faintest glow of thread.

"How did you do it?" I asked.

Gabby stood. She picked up her staff and threw the leather pack over her shoulder. "Shepherds can do all sorts of things." She winked.

"And what about the story?" I asked. "What happened after the girl and the wood-carver got married?"

"That, my child, is a tale to be told by another."

"*Baa*," said a sheep across the stream.

Gabby sighed. "It's time for me to go."

"Wait!" I cried, for I'd suddenly realized the significance of what had just taken place. Simon was healed, which meant he didn't need to go to the hospital. Which meant we could continue to search for the coin. I had to repay her.

I dug through my backpack, looking for a present. Two pairs of shorts, toothbrushes. Everything seemed either ridiculous or completely inadequate. Pepperoni slices were the best I could do. "Here," I said, holding up the bag, "this is for you."

"I can't take your food."

"I want to repay you."

"Then find my lamb."

And with that, the shepherdess floated across the stream to rejoin her flock.

Simon and I watched her walk among them. We watched until the great white, woolly mass and the solitary purple figure disappeared into a far-off wood.

"Cheese," Simon said sleepily.

Which can best be translated as this: "Now we are alone."

Chapter 15

Night was falling. **Gray light seeped through** the valley. The stream no longer sparkled like glass; its water was now dark and murky.

Simon and I sat on a log we'd rolled beneath a great white oak. Crystal rested beside us, legs folded gracefully under her body. Her beautiful mane, reflecting the last rays of sunlight, looked like spun gold. I'd taken off her saddle and bridle for the evening. Hope pecked along the water's edge, searching for one last morsel before the sun completely disappeared from view.

"I guess we'll camp here for the night." I was more than a bit disappointed. I had hoped, after Gabby left, that Simon and I might venture farther. But the silvery lotion she'd applied to his lips had made him so groggy that I was afraid if we were to continue, he might fall out of the saddle.

I spread the blanket I'd packed, then led Simon to the stream to brush his teeth. You could tell he wasn't quite right. He didn't even try to bite me when I brushed his molars. Instead, he stood docilely, mouth wide open, the perfect dental patient.

I laid him down on the blanket, then took off his shoes and scooped up Hope and placed her on his chest. I lay down beside him, hands behind my head. Crystal came closer. She stretched out her knobby legs beside me. I could smell her wild, warm scent and feel the heat radiating from her body.

The ground was hard and bumpy, but I wasn't tired anyway. So I watched the sky go black and the stars come into focus. Momma would be home now. Preparing for sleep, she'd find my letter on her pillow.

I tried to imagine what she thought, the moment she read it. But Momma's head was not an easy place to climb into or figure out. She might have been angry or worried or maybe so plain tired that she didn't care. But what I hoped she was was certain.

Certain I could do everything I promised.

The night was long, and I slept poorly. Owls called. Coyotes yipped. Twigs snapped. I was sure I heard footsteps. At each sound, my eyes shot open, and my heart tried to escape from my chest. Once, I promise you, I heard a serpent's deadly hiss, curling against my ear. There was no moon. Eyes open or closed, it didn't matter. All I could see was black.

When morning finally came, I was more tired than when the night began. But I was relieved, too—the birds and their heraldry were music to my ears. Simon had snuggled up against me in the night, and Hope had moved her perch to his head. Crystal was gone, grazing at the stream, I figured. Because I didn't want to wake Simon, I stayed where I was, welcoming the morning on my back.

That's why it took so long to find out what had happened.

Finally, Simon awoke, and Hope did him the favor of hopping off his head. He sat up and rubbed his eyes.

"Cheese," he said.

"I'm hungry, too. Let's have breakfast."

I went over to the oak tree, where I'd hung our backpacks on a limb so raccoons wouldn't get into them in the night. Only, our backpacks weren't there.

Looking around, I realized Crystal wasn't there, either.

"Simon," I yelled. "Help me."

We searched the area, all along the stream, through-out the trees. The backpacks were gone. But we did find Crystal. She was hiding about a football field away, in some bushes.

I felt so sick at the sight of her that I wanted to throw up.

Her mane, her beautiful golden mane, had been cut off. Her tail, too. Around her neck was a loop of twine. Attached to the twine was a piece of cardboard on which was written:

THE EGGS GO CRACK, CRACK, CRACK.

I pulled the sign off and threw it as far as I could.

Simon began to cry.

"Oh, Crystal," I choked out. Golden horsehair was scattered all over the ground, which meant Gordon hadn't even cut it off to sell it. He'd cut it only to be cruel.

Crystal stood with her head bent, her long neck sloping to the ground. She would not look up when I clicked my tongue. I realized she was ashamed of what he had done to her.

Without pausing to consider if my words were true, I said, "Sweet, sweet pony, do not worry. It's not your fault. You're still as pretty as the day we first saw you."

And as soon as I said it, I knew it was somehow true. Her flaxen mane lay in clumps on the ground, yet Crystal was as beautiful as ever. I put a hand to her muzzle and gently lifted her head. Her icy blue eyes were filled with enough sorrow to drown your heart.

I ran a hand down her forehead. "Trust me," I said, and led her back to the campsite.

There was no breakfast, Gordon having stolen our backpacks. All of our supplies were gone, too: flashlight, food, water bottles. Toothbrushes. Oh, how upset Momma would be if we ended up with cavities. If Hope was the kind of chicken who laid eggs, maybe we'd have something. But then again, maybe not. I had no way to cook an egg, and I couldn't imagine cracking one open and slipping its slimy contents into my mouth.

"Cheese?" Simon asked pitifully.

"There is no cheese. There is no nothing." I spoke more harshly than I intended, and Simon began to cry some more. I put an arm around his shoulders. Poor kid. He was just a soldier. I was the commander. But what I was feeling like was a failure. Crystal assaulted. All our stuff gone. And I was the one who let it happen. I shouldn't have slept. I should have kept watch through the night.

"Shoulda, woulda, coulda." That's what Momma said, so I said it, too. Then I folded up our blanket—the only thing we had left. I resaddled Crystal and set the blanket on top. Then Simon let out a squeal. He'd found his crown and scepter, where the blanket had been. It seemed we'd slept on them, which explained why the ground had been so bumpy.

"All right, King Cookie," I said, and boosted him onto Crystal's back. Then I handed him Hope and slipped the bridle over the pony's head.

We had no food, no supplies. Our party had been ambushed. But we moved forward undeterred, in search of the coin.

Ad astra per aspera.

To the stars through difficulties.

"Maybe we can find something to eat," I said as we trudged up a hill. I don't know why. What could we possibly find? Some poisonous berries? A dead squirrel? Perhaps I was feeling optimistic because I thought we'd hit rock bottom. So much bad had happened that we were due for some good. It couldn't get any worse, I thought.

I was wrong.

The sky was gray that morning. The wind whistled with foreboding. But we walked on, oblivious.

"Cheese," Simon said.

"I'm thirsty, too." We'd come to the top of the hill. Before us was an endless sea of prairie grass, tall as Crystal's shoulders. Down a slope to our right was a green field. To the left was forest, dense and dark.

I'd been avoiding the forest; I'm sure you've figured that out. I did not believe in witches, or goblins, or trolls—but if they did exist, the woods were where they'd make their home. That was obvious. It was obvious, too, though, that if I was hoping to find a cave, it would not be plopped down in the middle of a prairie.

Crystal wanted no part of it. She stood, hooves firmly planted at the forest's edge, and tossed her head.

"Come on, girl." I pulled at her reins.

She blinked an icy eye and snorted.

I wondered if she knew something. If she could see a

man with amber eyes, crouching among the branches. If she did, and if she could, she didn't tell me. So I tugged, and finally she put one white leg into the shadows.

There wasn't a trail, so we cut our way between limbs, over fallen trees, through thistles and nettles. I had the sinking feeling as we slowly made our way through the forest that we were lost—really lost—and every step we took led us farther from familiar land. There was a tickling at the back of my mind, an awful, omnipresent whisper: *Lost and gone forever.* Yet I chose to continue. My heart held tight to the promise of the cave.

The canopy of leaves overhead was green and thick, which is why I didn't notice the rain at first. And even once I did notice it, I didn't care.

"Just a sprinkle," I told Simon. "We won't feel a thing in here."

Hope let out a cackle, which in retrospect was a warning, but since I didn't speak chicken, I misunderstood.

"See, Simon, even Hope agrees: A little rain never hurt anybody."

And then the forest suddenly turned gray, as if someone had switched off a light. There was a great gust of wind that bent the trees. Then it began to pour. I mean, really pour. It was unlike anything I'd ever seen. Water fell from the sky in curtains and with such force that I could barely stand.

"Cheese!" Simon cried in dismay.

Crystal sank to her knees. Hope tucked in her neck, becoming a feathery ball.

I didn't know what to do. Thunder shook the forest floor, like an earthquake. The rain was so heavy that I had to squint. In a few short seconds, I had become completely drenched. But there was nowhere to go. Nowhere to seek shelter. We were trapped.

"Come on, girl, don't give up!" I had to yell to be heard over the downpour as I pulled at Crystal's reins.

Head bowed, she refused to budge.

Simon was sobbing. His felt crown had slipped down around his neck.

"Help!" I screamed in desperation. "Somebody please help!"

It was then that the log cabin appeared, not fifty feet in front of us. I don't know how I missed it before. A lamp burned warm yellow in its window.

I gave the pony a mighty tug. Finally, she lifted onto her feet. Simon still crying, we trudged through the pouring rain toward that glowing lamp.

Before I could knock, the cabin door swung open with a great gust.

A monster stood in the entry.

Chapter 16

It might have been a demon, actually. I don't really know how to tell the difference. Its face was red, its eyes yellow, its blue lips curled in a sneer. Atop its head, two purple horns twisted, scaly as serpents.

What I do know is that I screamed a scream so loud and full of fright that it put all my previous screams to shame. Simon screamed, too. Crystal reared up on her back legs, nearly causing Simon to slide off the saddle.

"That has to be the loudest hello-sir-may-we-seek-shelter-in-your-humble-abode that I've ever heard," the monster/demon said.

Then it tore off its face. "Even so, please come in."

The monster had morphed into a man with a handlebar mustache and pointy beard.

I stayed where I was, in the rain.

"There's nothing to be afraid of," he said. "It's just a mask." He shook the mask a little, as if to prove it. "Unless you enjoy being out of doors during a torrential downpour?" He stepped back into the shadows without waiting for an answer.

"The pony can come in, too," he called.

So we entered.

The cabin was small, just a single room with a mini-fridge and the tiniest of stoves. The bathroom was the size of a closet. But there was a fireplace with a roaring fire and a big, blue braided rug to spread out on, which the four of us did. The man took our wet blanket and draped it on a chair to dry. He propped Simon's crown and scepter near the fireplace grate. Then he took a seat in a rocking chair. His mask hung from a hook on the wall beside him.

He saw me looking at it.

"There are nasty characters in these parts. Under certain circumstances, a face like that can come in handy."

He meant Gordon. I was sure of it.

"Didn't Sister Melanie warn you?"

"You know Sister Melanie?"

The man rubbed one of the curls of his mustache. "You're Perpetua, right?"

I nodded.

"You can call me A.R." He stuck out a hand, and I took it. A warm wave washed over my body.

"Are you hungry?" he asked.

The rain had made me forget that we'd had no breakfast, that we had no lunch, that there was no hope for dinner. Before I could answer, A.R. got out of his chair. He went to his little kitchen area and came back carrying a tray. On it were six yellow bowls and two glasses of water.

A.R. set the tray on the rug and began to hand out dishes. To both Simon and me, he gave a glass and a bowl of meaty stew. For our animal companions, he set out two bowls apiece: water and oats for Crystal, water and dry rice for Hope.

I was so hungry that I dug right in, not even considering how it was possible that this stranger would have ready the exact nourishment each of us needed. I was so hungry that I didn't care some of the vegetables looked like algae and there were tiny fish bodies floating in the broth. Simon ate up, too, without even a nose wrinkle—which was actually a bigger miracle than A.R.'s waiting food tray.

I finished and set my empty bowl on the tray, then stretched out my legs, basking in the dry warmth of the fire. I could feel A.R. watching me, but it wasn't a creepy kind of watching. He was waiting, I knew, for me to speak.

So I thought of a question, a question which I should have asked Gabby, which I'm sure I would've asked her if I hadn't been so worried about Simon's lip. "Do you know where a cave is around here?"

"No," A.R. said.

That figured.

"You're disappointed," he said. "I can tell."

I shrugged and kept my eyes on the fire. He was right, though. I was disappointed. I guess I'd been hoping that, just this once, something could be easy.

"Would you like me to tell you a story?"

The answer, quite simply, was no. What I would have liked to do was join my three companions in a nap. Crystal's eyes were closed, Hope had her head tucked in, and Simon was lying between them, a thumb in his mouth. But A.R. had prevented us from starving, so I owed him. And I couldn't offer him a bag of pepperoni, as I had Gabby. All I had were my ears.

Sister Melanie said that every time you did something you didn't want to do but ought to, it was like a payment toward a great big good in the future. When I told Momma that, she said, "I'd prefer cash money right here and now, thank you very much."

But what I wondered was if there was a way to have both: future and present good, all wrapped up together.

"Yes, tell it to me," I said.

A.R. nodded and stroked his pointy beard. "Let's see. Where should I begin? Once upon a time, there was a world, a big, beautiful world. And in this world was a family. The family was poor—monetarily, at least. The father was a janitor; the mother stayed home. They had

one child, a son, and lived in a trailer, where they had to work hard to acquire their few belongings.

"The boy didn't mind being poor. He lived in a small town where everyone had drawn the same lot. His birthdays and Christmases were simple affairs— but so were everyone else's. Because his family had little money, he'd not been taught to love wealth. As such, he was content, for he didn't long for what he didn't have.

"He spent his days exploring the woods behind the trailer park. He'd catch crawdads in the creek and swing from tree branches. He spent every hour he could in the outdoors, and he was happy. There was just one problem: school.

"He was no good at school, so he hated it. And that makes sense. Who can enjoy something they fail at? And fail he did, year after year. His spelling was atrocious, he had difficulty reading, and trying to compose a paragraph brought him to tears.

"Now, had his family been well-off, they would have hired specialists and tutors to help the boy. The truth was, the boy was incredibly bright. His struggles had nothing to do with his intelligence. With some specialized instruction, he could have gotten A's with the rest of them. Alas, this was not to be.

"He was put in the not-fit-for-school class and largely forgotten. He gave up trying to succeed. His hands, having rejected pen and paper, searched for something else to hold on to.

"He turned to knives. Whittling knives, to be exact. In the woods, he'd find branches and whittle away until he held something magnificent in his hands: a tulip, a rosebud, a grapevine. It wasn't long before his mother had a veritable garden on the kitchen windowsill to gaze at while she washed the dishes.

"The boy practiced, and his work got better: the cuts smoother, the details more elaborate. He moved to bigger pieces and longer knives. The summer he was sixteen, he mowed yards all around the trailer park and saved enough money to buy a chain saw.

"Now he found his true passion. His carvings quadrupled in size. He was making statues. Word spread throughout town. Folks lined up to watch him work. He started taking custom orders. He saved enough money to buy a car. It was a rusty old station wagon, but it was a car.

"The day he graduated from high school, he loaded up the station wagon with everything he owned (which could fit in a single cardboard box, minus the chain saw), kissed his teary-eyed mother, and shook his surprised father's hand. He was heading west, with a plan to spend the summer putting on a chain-saw carving demonstration at every fair he passed.

"Where he ended up—after many weeks and nearly a dozen fairs—was California, in a pretty town with palm trees, not far from the ocean. He was in the middle of a demonstration—carving a Pegasus out of an enormous block of wood, which he then planned to auction off to the highest bidder—when a figure in the crowd caught his eye. It was a girl. She looked sad and kind of lost. (She was both.) Her strawberry-blond hair fell to her elbows. He couldn't stop looking at her, which was pretty dangerous, since he was operating a chain saw.

"As soon as the Pegasus was finished, the boy went over to her. He forgot to take off his safety goggles. The girl laughed in his face.

" 'Who are you under there?' she asked.

"The boy raised the goggles, and the girl stopped laughing. Something passed between them, a pop of electricity that changed their destinies.

" 'Now I see you,' the girl said."

A.R. stopped speaking. He rocked silently in his chair.

"Well?" I said. "What happened next?"

"They fell in love, of course. Two weeks later, they were married in the simplest of ceremonies. The boy carved a beautiful box shaped like an infinity symbol, inside which was the ring he presented to his bride.

"The girl's mother was furious. The boy's parents

were delighted. So they moved to where they were welcome, to a small town in Iowa. There they lived, nearly poor, but quite happy, for a long time. Until one day—"

A.R. suddenly stopped speaking again.

"Until one day what?" I asked.

He twirled the ends of his mustache. "Well, what happened next is part of a different story." He got up and stoked the fire. "Are you dry now?"

I realized I was. I realized, too, that the rain had stopped, for I could no longer hear it battering the roof.

Simon slowly rose from his sleeping position on the floor. As if on cue, Hope stood up and flapped her wings, adjusting her feathers. Crystal rose, too. She tossed her head, flinging the last drops of water from her stubby mane.

It was time to go.

I got Simon's crown and placed it on his head, put the scepter in his hand. I turned to say goodbye to A.R. but found the red-faced monster standing in his place.

I didn't scream this time. "Thank you for helping us," I said, and shook the monster's outstretched hand. A wave of warmth again swept over my body.

"Remember," A.R. said. "Appearances can be deceiving."

"I know. I've read a lot of fairy tales."

"Ah, then you are wise in the ways that matter."

I led my traveling companions outside, into a forest where the sun's rays pierced through the branches. The leaves were covered in sparkling raindrops. I helped Simon onto Crystal's saddle, then adjusted Hope till she looked comfortable in his arms.

We had walked fifty yards when I remembered the blanket, hanging over A.R.'s chair. "We'll have to go back," I told Simon. "We might need it."

But when I turned around, the cabin was no longer there.

Chapter 17

We walked aimlessly for a long time. I couldn't decide what to do. We were out of food; we had no supplies. The sensible thing would be to try to find our way home. But a part of me—a big part—didn't want to do the sensible thing. What I wanted, still, was to find the coin.

The forest floor was so muddy that Crystal's legs turned black. My shoes were caked in mud so thick it felt like I was wearing blocks of cement. So I did something that would prove to be pretty foolish. I took my shoes off, tied the laces together, and swung them over my shoulder. Mud oozed up between my toes.

I kept an eye out for a cave, but there was no cave, only forest. And soon we were out of the forest. We'd come to a flat, green field with a barbed wire fence around it and a red metal gate.

"Cheese?" Simon asked.

"I see no reason we shouldn't." I opened the gate, and we walked into the field. This was the second foolish thing I did that afternoon.

We were making our way across the field when I first heard the thunder—or what I thought was thunder. It came rumbling through the earth like a tremor. Pausing, I surveyed the landscape, expecting to see clouds on the horizon. But the sky was clear, a beautiful swimming-pool blue. And so it was not clouds I saw, but cattle. An entire herd of them, running in our direction.

Now, I knew nothing about cows, only that the nuns allowed a herd to graze on their pasture. Sister Melanie on many occasions had slipped us a pound or two of hamburger.

"Cheese?" Simon said, which meant, "Should we be worried that enormous, thousand-pound animals are running toward us at full speed?"

"I don't know," I said.

The cattle ran closer. And when they were maybe thirty feet away, they stopped. Their massive brown bodies formed a line, and they stood staring at us with impenetrable, glassy eyes. Their muzzles were yellow-white, and they had plastic tags in their ears. Heads lowered, they stood, as if waiting for the sign to charge.

And then the sign was given.

The biggest cow, which stood in the middle of the herd, lifted its head toward the sky and bellowed. The line charged at the command.

I had only a moment, enough time to utter a single word. "Run!" I yelled, then let go of Crystal's reins. That pony took off so fast you'd have thought she was a contender in the Kentucky Derby. I knew she, Simon, and Hope would be safe.

As for me, I did not have equine speed. So I chose not to run, but stood right where I was, bare, mud-caked feet planted in the pasture. Within seconds, the bovine wave swept over me. I was no sturdier than a scarecrow under their massive force. I fell almost immediately and was trampled.

This is what I remember: legs, hooves, and a *moo-*ing so loud and deep that it resonated in my muscles. I closed my eyes and tried to roll myself into a ball. I felt the cattle's beastly heat and rough fur brushing against my body. And then I felt the sharp snap of my bone.

And suddenly it was over. The cows were past. I lay on the ground. All was quiet. I was alone. Carefully I rolled onto my back. I could feel each spot where the hooves had hit. And my arm—my poor broken arm. I started to cry because it hurt so bad that I couldn't stand to move it. The pain radiated in waves, spreading across my body. It was all I could do not to scream.

I never knew pain could make you go crazy. But crazy is what I felt like, tears streaming down my face, hurt radiating from my bone. I started having visions. Crystal appeared above me, all fuzzy white, like an angel, and blew warm air over my brow. Then Simon showed up. He knelt by my shoulders and with trembling lips offered me his crown. Next, it was Gabby, in her shepherd's robe. She was holding her little lost lamb. And then came A.R., in the red monster mask. He leaned down so close that his purple horns brushed my hair.

"Boo!" he yelled.

My eyes flew open, and I stared up at that swimming-pool sky.

I thought of my daddy, in bed with his busted arm.

"I'm just like him now," I said.

And then everything went black.

Chapter 18

I woke, foggy-brained, to a man above me. He looked familiar, but I couldn't place him or his furry sideburns. There was something almost mesmerizing about the blaze of his amber eyes.

He was talking, but I was unable to hear him. It felt like I was underwater and the sound couldn't reach my ears. Suddenly, he gripped my shoulders and shook me. Pain shot through my body.

"*Ooww,*" I yelped.

"Girl, are you listening?"

I could hear him now.

"Girl, I want to help you, but you've got to pay attention."

That seemed an impossible task. Though I could

now hear the man's words, it still felt like I was underwater. The world was wavy and slow. And the pain— the pain of my broken arm took up almost all the space in my head. I suddenly knew how Daddy felt. When your body fails you, there's not much room for anything else. I didn't know where I was, and I couldn't remember how I'd got here.

The man held up a silver circle between his fingers. "Look, girl. I found it."

"Found what?"

"The coin," he growled. "The coin you were looking for."

Coin? Why was I looking for a coin? An image suddenly flashed above the pain: a basket of eggs, all of them cracked.

He lifted my good arm and pressed the coin into my palm. "I want you to have it."

"Have what?"

"The coin," he breathed through gritted teeth.

I tried to think what, exactly, a coin was, and what I might do with it.

The man seemed to read my mind. "You can use it to help your family. Sell it for a whole bunch of money."

"Okay," I said, still not knowing what he was talking about. My arm throbbed, and the world undulated around me.

"Aren't I good?" the man asked. "To give you the coin?"

I nodded. It did seem good to give somebody something—even if you weren't sure what the something was that you were being given.

"So you can stop looking, then, right? I gave you the coin, so you can go on home."

That seemed sensible. Once you'd found the thing you were supposedly looking for, you didn't need to look for it anymore.

The man leaned down so close that his head blocked out the sky. "You're done searching, right?"

"Right."

"You promise?"

"Promise."

The man smiled unpleasantly. "Good."

And it might have been the pain, messing up my mind, but I'll tell you what I saw: The man's face changed into a wolf's, sharp-toothed and hungry. Then, just as quickly, it changed back.

The man looked around, got up, walked away, then came back. He held a pair of muddy tennis shoes whose laces had been tied together. "I'm going to take these," he said. "In exchange for the coin. Deal?"

"Deal," I murmured. What use could I have for someone's muddy shoes?

That ferocious smile spread across his face.

Somewhere in my mind, a woman's timid voice said, "Oh dear."

"Now go on home," the man said. "Get out of here."

"I don't think I can stand."

"Get up!" he shouted. He grabbed my broken arm and tugged.

I screamed. The pain was more than I could bear.

He put his face right up against mine. His eyes seemed to ripple. "I'll give you to the count of ten, girl. If you're not up—" He pulled a knife from his pocket and pointed the blade at my nose.

There was a buzzing sound then, like a swarm of bees hovering overhead. An instant later, an arrow shot out of nowhere and landed in the man's hand.

He let out a terrific howl. The knife he'd been holding fell to the ground as he leapt up and began to jump around, the arrow sticking straight out from the back of his hand.

"Leave her alone," a voice boomed.

It was unlike any voice I'd ever heard—so loud and big. It seemed to be coming from everywhere at once—both falling from the sky and rising from the earth.

I watched the man look around in all directions, till he must have seen the speaker. I could not see him, though, because he was some distance behind where I lay on the grass.

The man stopped howling. His face turned white, and his mouth froze in a horrified O. He grabbed his knife and the muddy shoes and ran.

The enormous voice laughed. "HA! HA! HA! I love it when they scurry like vermin."

I still couldn't see the speaker, though I could hear the great thud of his footsteps as he drew closer. I wasn't afraid. Maybe I should have been. But there was something *good*—I could sense it—in that enormous voice, in those mighty steps.

I stared up at the blue sky as I waited for him. I imagined I was in a swimming pool, both of my arms strong and healthy as I swam lap after lap.

"Are you all right, little miss?" The voice was beside my head. Finally, I could see its owner.

He was a giant.

I really do mean that. The man was gigantic. He was the largest human I'd ever seen. If my big, strong daddy stood beside him, Daddy would look like a child. This man was over seven feet tall, and his chest stuck out like a barrel. He had a short, blond beard and long, blond hair that fell to his shoulders in waves. His face was rough. His eyes sparkled green. He wore pants and a leather tunic. Over one shoulder hung a quiver of arrows. He held a wooden bow in his hand.

"Are you all right?" he boomed again.

My body vibrated with his words, which sent another wave of pain through my limbs. "Not really," I gasped.

"Good thing I'm here, then," he said. He crouched his enormous frame beside me. "My name's Mike, by the way. Don't be afraid."

And then he lifted me, with arms as thick as telephone poles, into the air.

Chapter 19

There was darkness, even though my eyes were open. There was a feeling of flight, even though I could hear Mike's feet as they hit the ground. He was running, and I was in his arms, and even though my bone was broken and I didn't know

how to find my way home, I felt the safest I'd ever felt. In Mike's arms, I knew nothing could hurt me; therefore, there was nothing to fear.

He ran for what seemed a long time. Wind kissed my face and blew my hair. "Where are we going?" I tried to ask, but my lips wouldn't form the words. So I was quiet, and Mike was quiet, save the heavy breaths that escaped from his chest.

Finally, we stopped moving. And then it was as if a great overhead light was turned on. I could see again.

We were at a campsite in the woods. There was a firepit, a wooden bench, and a string of lights between the trees. Mike set me down on the bench. The instant I was upright, my mind defogged. I thought of several things all at the same time, but the most important was Simon. I'd sent Crystal running with my brother on her back, and now I didn't know where he was.

I thought again of the letter I'd written, how I'd promised Momma and Daddy that I would take care of my brother. Now he was lost, which meant I'd lied, even though I hadn't meant to. Tears spilled from my eyes.

"Why do you cry, little miss?" Mike asked. He'd removed his quiver and arrows and now crouched, looking boulder-like, beside the firepit.

"I lost the person I was supposed to care for," I told

him, tears salty on my lips. My broken arm throbbed, but it was nothing compared to the ache in my chest.

"I see." Mike brought two big fingers to his mouth. The whistle that came out was long and high-pitched. I imagined the sound slicing through the woods for miles.

Then there was quiet.

Then there was a horse's neigh.

Crystal stepped out from behind some trees on the other side of the campsite. My brother was on her back.

Never had I been so happy to see that Cookie Boy in all my life. I stumbled toward him and his beloved chicken, which sat on his lap.

"I found those three wandering in a clearing," Mike said. "Couldn't make heads or tails out of anything the little guy said, but from the looks of the pony, it seemed there'd been trouble."

"Cheese," Simon agreed.

I laughed, squeezing his leg, and petted what was left of Crystal's mane. Then I frowned. Part of what I'd thought of when my mind had defogged concerned this pony and what had been done to her. Gordon, I now remembered, was the one who had hurt her and robbed us. He was the one who had pointed a knife at my nose and taken my shoes.

I realized I still held the coin he'd given me in my palm. Slowly, I raised it. I could see the grooves of a foil wrapper. Using my thumb and forefinger, I pressed as hard as I could. The coin snapped in half.

It was made of chocolate. I let the pieces fall to the ground.

I helped Simon down from the pony, and he set Hope loose to scavenge for insects. Mike was by the firepit. He'd laid out a bed of coals, which glowed orange. He had a metal grate over the top of them and a cooking pot.

"Have a seat," he called. "Dinner is about to be served."

I led Simon to the wooden bench. We watched Mike pour the contents of the pot into two silver thermoses. He handed one to each of us, then stood back, crossed his arms, and smiled.

"Bon appétit," he boomed.

I brought the thermos to my lips with my good arm. The liquid was warm. I don't know how to describe its taste except to say it was like drinking gold. There was a hint of chicken and rosemary, cream and carrots. It was the best broth I'd ever tasted. Simon and I both drank it greedily, without speaking.

Mike laughed when we had finished and handed him our empty thermoses. "I see my cooking has met your expectations."

"Thank you. That was delicious," I said.

"*Chee—eese,*" agreed Simon.

Mike made a true fire now, with flames and crackling logs. All of us watched it for a moment, Simon and I sitting, Mike standing a little way off, massive arms crossed. He cast glances at me, as if wondering when I'd ask the question I held in my head.

Finally, I said, "Is it wrong to break a promise?"

"Little miss, I suspect you already know the answer to that."

He was right. I asked a different question. "Can you break a promise based on a lie?"

"Let me see." Mike rubbed his bearded chin. "What I think I hear you asking is this: If Gordon, taking advantage of your confused mental state, got you to promise you'd go home, are you obliged to stop searching for the coin? Is that what you're asking?"

I looked at him with equal parts fear and awe. How did he know? And then a different question formed in my mind, one that made me tremble even though I didn't understand it: What was this entity who stood before me?

"No," Mike said, even though I hadn't answered him. "You don't have to stop searching. Under no circumstances should you honor a lie."

I nodded, relieved.

"And just as an aside—Gordon will never find the coin."

"How do you know?"

"The poem says so." Mike cleared his throat and straightened his back, as if about to give a classroom recitation. "*Though the cave be dark and dreary / little ones won't grow weary*. Does Gordon strike you as a little one?"

I couldn't help but laugh.

"Yeah, me neither," said Mike. Then he paused. "No, Gordon won't *find* the coin, but that doesn't mean he won't *possess* it."

The laughter instantly dried in my throat. Even though I didn't know exactly what Mike meant, I knew enough to feel uneasy.

"But, on the other hand, I don't know how much luck *you're* going to have finding it, either. Being one-armed and barefooted, I mean."

"He took my shoes," I said.

"Unfortunately, I am not a cobbler."

"My arm was trampled by a herd of cattle."

"Ah—now that may be something I can help with. I was just waiting for you to ask."

"Did I ask?"

Mike's green eyes flashed. "Close enough."

In his quiver, there was a small bronze box. In the box was a roll of silver-flecked gauze. Mike unrolled it.

"I didn't know that bowmen were trained as medics," I said.

"Arrows are my specialty, it's true. But bandages are a close second. Now hold out your arm."

"I can't."

"Simon," Mike said.

Very carefully, my brother lifted my arm. Even still, I winced.

"Close your eyes," Mike said.

I obeyed, and down at my wrist he began to wrap. I bit my lip. I will not say it was torture, but I will say the level of pain was just one house over. To distract myself, I said, "What do you hunt?"

"Oh, anything wild and wicked that has no place here."

I thought of the arrow shot through Gordon's hand. "Does that include humans?"

Mike was quiet, wrapping. Then he said, "If necessary."

"Do the sisters know you roam about their land?" I couldn't decide what they'd think of this gigantic man and his quiver of arrows. I couldn't decide what I thought of him, either.

"They are aware of my presence, yes." Mike touched a finger to my collar. "Open your eyes."

My arm was enclosed, from wrist to shoulder, in silvery shimmer. It did not feel better—it felt like nothing at all. It felt like my arm was missing and I had a left hand that floated independent of my body. I turned my arm this way and that, feeling nothing, and watched the silver gauze reflect the sun's dying rays. Something about the sparkle reminded me of the lotion that had been applied to my brother's lip.

"Do you know Gabby, the shepherdess?" I asked.

"Never heard of her," Mike said. "But if you find that little lost lamb, be sure to let me know."

I stared at him. He winked.

"Are you ready for a story?" he asked, and sat down on the bench in the space between me and Simon. His giant form completely obstructed my brother from view.

"Will you start where the others left off?"

"I'll start at the beginning, which, in my experience, is always the best place to begin."

I must have made a face, though I didn't mean to, because he leaned toward me and added, "Don't worry. You'll like it."

"How do you know?"

Mike laughed. "HA! HA! HA!" Three great thunder booms. "Everyone likes to hear stories about themselves."

My heart leapt a little. "I'm in it?"

"You're in it."

"Cheese?" asked Simon from somewhere on the other side of Mike.

"You, too, cheddar lover."

"Please," I said, "then let's begin."

"Once upon a time?" Mike asked.

I nodded. "Once upon a time . . ."

Chapter 20

There was a world, a big, beautiful world. And in this world was a couple—a man who carved wood and a woman who'd lost much—who lived simply, in the countryside. They had a garden, the greenest and lushest you'd ever seen, which the woman had cultivated, seed by seed, with her two wild hands. They were happy. But something was missing."

"A child?" I asked because, as I had told A.R., I had read a lot of fairy tales.

"That's right. A child. A child is always what is missing. And so when the child finally arrived, the couple was delighted.

"The baby was a girl. The mother wrapped her in a pink swaddling blanket and laid her in a cradle the father had built during the long months when they awaited her arrival.

"The baby grew strong and healthy. Soon she could crawl, and then walk. They put up an enclosure in the yard, where she could play while her father carved and be safe from flying wood chips and sawdust.

"The baby kept growing. She grew hair and teeth. As her body became taller, her mind became smarter. She could speak and sing and count, and then read. Her mother taught her how to identify every vegetable in the garden. When the girl was five, a big yellow bus stopped in front of her house, waiting to take her to a place where she would grow even more, in preparation for her journey in the world.

"Yes, the baby—no longer a baby—was happy. And her parents were happy. But something was missing."

"Another child!" I couldn't help but cry, and smiled in Simon's direction, even though I couldn't see him.

"That's right. It's always a child. A boy this time, as dark-haired as the girl was light. The baby grew. He learned all the things his sister had learned. Soon, he was a toddler. He was as talkative as a parakeet and as mischievous as a monkey. The mother was happy. The father was happy. The girl and boy were happy, too. Life was good and sweet, as it often is.

"And then something happened.

"On a windy day, the father fell from high atop a ladder. When he hit the ground, the family lost nearly everything they possessed. The father could not carve, the boy could not speak, the mother could not rest. And the girl, who blamed herself for what had happened, couldn't figure out how to fix it.

"Life was bad and bitter, as it sometimes is.

"The father had one surgery, then a second. There was no money for a third. Things went from bad to worse. Vines withered, faith vanished, hope dried up. 'Things will never get better,' the wind whispered. 'Tomorrow is lost.'

"The wind was so loud, its message so persistent, that the family began to repeat its message, not with their lips, but in their hearts: *Things will never get better. Tomorrow is lost.*

"Only the girl refused to believe it. And because she refused, she was the only one who could see the way out, how to get back to before. Her father needed another surgery, for which they needed money, for which she had to find a coin. She could fix everything, she knew, if she could only find it."

"But she was just a child," I interjected.

"She wasn't *just* anything," Mike thundered. "She was tough, and brave, and smart. And being a child was no disadvantage. Quite the contrary. Because she was young, her heart had not hardened. That was how she could *feel*. And that is how she *knew*.

"So she packed her things. She took what she needed. Then she headed down into the valley."

Mike stopped. The sky had lost its color. Night was falling.

"Then what happened?" I asked.

"She ran into trouble, of course. There were accidents and injuries. Thieving and fights. There were helpers, too. Bright beacons of light. So every time she thought of quitting, she chose instead to continue."

Mike stood up, stretched his arms, and arched his back. "Man, I'm tired."

I could finally see Simon again. He had curled up on the bench and was almost asleep.

"So?" I said.

"So what?"

"Did the girl find the coin?"

Mike smiled. His green eyes flashed. "I don't know. You tell me. You're the one writing the story."

Chapter 21

"Y ou can camp here tonight," Mike said. He had a tarp he was tying between two trees to make a shelter. "I'll keep watch."

The sky had finished fading and was now the deep gray of a pigeon. The fire glowed yellow orange against the night.

"You got a blanket?" Mike asked.

"We lost it."

"Good. It'll make you stronger to go without." Mike flexed an arm and winked. His bicep was as big as a bowling ball.

My own arm, the broken one, hung weightless at my side. It was hard not to be dejected by its uselessness. Another picture of my daddy, so sad in his bed, flashed in my mind. *I love you,* I whispered in my heart, and then I pushed him away. There was no time for self-pity right now. I had to choose something different.

Since we didn't have toothbrushes, I made Simon hold out his finger and rub it on his teeth. This wasn't even in the same category as brushing, but at least I could tell Momma we'd tried.

I led Simon to the tarp, and we lay down under it, on the grass. I folded my good arm behind my head and used my palm for a pillow. Crystal and Hope came over and settled down beside us.

It was dark enough now for the lightning bugs to come out. We watched them flash and glow fuzzy yellow as they floated in the air.

Mike stood some distance away, near the campfire. His figure loomed massive in the orange glow of the flames. He wore his quiver and held his bow at the ready. He turned his head slowly, scanning the horizon in all directions, like an eagle looking for prey.

Even though the ground was hard and coyotes yipped in the distance, I knew I'd sleep soundly. I knew Mike would protect us from whatever creatures prowled in the night. As long as the big man and his bow were present, I had nothing to fear.

"Tomorrow we'll find it," I whispered to Simon. I

don't know why. Maybe it's because I felt peaceful and sleepy. Maybe it's because I knew he must be missing Momma and Daddy pretty badly. I missed them, too.

He didn't say anything in reply. When I listened harder, I could hear how rhythmic his breathing was. He'd already fallen asleep.

I was only a few seconds from joining him, but in my final moments of consciousness, I thought about the coin. I tried to summon the cave.

I awoke in the morning to a chicken's cackle. The sky was the color of smoke. The rising sun painted the horizon with a strip of brilliant pink. I sat up. Crystal and Simon slept soundly on either side of me. The grass was wet with dew, the fire a pile of ashes.

Mike was gone.

Hope was on the other side of the firepit, near a bush dotted with poisonous red berries. She was still cackling like the soloist in a choir. I went over to her.

"What's wrong with you, silly bird? Why are you trying to wake everyone up?"

She looked at me, blinked her avian eyes, and then let loose a cackle that nearly split my eardrums.

I happened to look down.

There, in the wet grass, was an egg. Its shell was bread-loaf brown.

"Did you lay that?"

I promise this is the truth: That chicken looked at me and nodded.

I picked the egg up with my good arm. It was warm and perfectly smooth in my hand. I looked at Hope. I don't know if it's possible for chickens to feel proud, but if it is, then she certainly was. She smoothed her speckled feathers and tossed her head. She had finally done what chickens are supposed to do, and she seemed to think it the most terrific of accomplishments.

I didn't know what to do with the egg, so I just stood there, holding it as the sun inched upward, broadening the pink swath in the sky.

Out of the corner of my eye, something flashed white.

I turned my head. Nothing was there.

But somehow I knew—even without seeing.

"You stay here," I told Hope. "Keep an eye on Simon."

There was a grove of evergreens to my left. I

headed into them, feet bare, holding an egg, left arm disappeared. Since the sun had not yet reached its full height, the wooded area was dim. The ground was cool. Goose bumps danced across my skin.

Up ahead, white flashed between the evergreens.

Now the ground became inclined and rocky. I leaned forward a little, and the strain felt good because it warmed my body.

I didn't know how I would catch the lamb once I found it. I knew nothing of the ways of sheep, but I was pretty certain I couldn't just whistle and expect it to come prancing along at my heels, like a dog. But I didn't think too much about that. I just walked, heart jumping with excitement.

The path seemed to go on forever, and the incline became steeper. The rocks were sharper, too. I winced, but didn't dare pause to check the status of my feet. If my soles were bloody, I didn't want to know. *"Excelsior,"* I whispered.

Ever higher.

I kept my thoughts focused on the capture of the lamb. It felt like by returning it to Gabby, I'd be paying her back for fixing Simon's lip—and not just her, but A.R. and Mike, too. Somehow, in my mind, they'd all become linked. So by helping Gabby, I would help the others. By paying back one debt, I could repay them all.

"That's just silly, Pet," I could almost hear Momma's voice say.

"It might be silly, Momma," I whispered, "but it's true."

I stopped. My chest felt tight, and my lungs burned. The path had come to an end. I was at the top of a steep hill. In front of me was gray-brown limestone that stretched like a wall as far as I could see. If I lifted my gaze, I could make out the rock formation's top, which was dotted with scraggly trees. I didn't see a lamb up there, though, nor did I see one down where I was, either.

I stood, unsure what to do. There were tiger lilies growing at the rock's base, their orange petals curving delicately toward the ground. It was while bending to smell one that I noticed it.

An opening in the rock wall.

It is not an exaggeration to say that my heart began to beat so fast and hard that I thought I might lift into the air, like a helicopter.

Right there, in front of me, was the entrance of a cave.

Chapter 22

Caves are dark and wet, and this one was no exception. I had no flashlight or shoes. I couldn't see, and my feet felt frozen, stepping through the cool water. I inched forward, taking toddler-size steps. The air smelled like snow and was so cool that my teeth began to chatter. I could hear the steady drip of water.

I tried not to think about the creatures that dwell in caves: bats, snakes, insects born blind and white because they never see the sun. A part of me found it hard to believe that a little lost lamb would seek shelter in a place so dreary. Another part believed it wholeheartedly.

I don't know how deep into the cave I went.

Deep enough to think about Simon and worry that I shouldn't have left him with only a pony and a chicken for protection. Deep enough to worry I might find myself hundreds of feet belowground, utterly and completely lost.

Then the air changed. It became fuller somehow, and the tunnel was wider—this I could sense even though all I could see was dark. I paused, listening. There was that steady drip of water. And maybe something else.

My feet were so cold that they felt disappeared, like my arm. I still held Hope's egg, which had grown as cool as a stone. I listened. Drip . . . Drip . . . And something more. Breaths?

"Is somebody in here?" I asked. My voice echoed, small and crackly, as if covered in ice.

And then the most amazing thing happened. The cave filled with light.

High, high above me there was an opening in the rock. Through this opening, brilliant rays poured down, illuminating the cave in a soft, glimmering glow. I could now see quite clearly. And what I saw was astounding.

I was standing in a domed room. Stalactites hung from the ceiling. The white crystals were everywhere and looked like icicles. I felt like I was in a church, staring up in wonder. Like I was in one of those cathedrals whose ceilings arch toward heaven and are filled with paintings of clouds and angels. The paintings here were made of water and calcium, but they were just as breathtaking.

The most breathtaking thing of all, though, wasn't above, but in front of me. There was a pool of water so clear that I could see my reflection in it. And on the other side of the pool, a part of the cave jutted out, like a platform.

On the platform stood a lamb.

The lamb was the most beautiful creature I had ever laid eyes on. Its wool seemed to be tinged with silver threads. Its hooves shone as if polished. The fleece on its face looked soft as velvet, and its eyes were dark as ink with flecks of gold.

"No wonder Gabby has been searching for you," I said. "If you were mine, I would never let you go."

The lamb lifted one polished hoof and clicked it against the limestone platform. Then it turned its head and looked right at me.

Its teeth flashed silver.

A shiver flew up my spine. I took a step forward and my toes touched the cool edge of the crystal-clear pool. Though I knew nothing about lambs, I did know this: Their teeth aren't made of silver.

"What do you have?" I asked.

"*Baa,*" said the lamb.

I waded into the pool. Though the water was clear, I could not see its bottom, which meant it was deep. But that was okay. I knew how to swim.

It wasn't until I'd waded up to my waist that I realized my predicament. Yes, I knew how to swim, but not with a broken arm and while holding an egg.

I paused in the water, which had grown warmer the farther in I'd waded, and considered what I should do. The lamb kept its inky eyes on me, curious but silent.

Now this, I think, might be the most magnificent part of all. I began to move. Not float or swim, but just move. As if my body were a boat, I cut through the water. I glided as smooth as a knife slicing through warm butter.

When I reached the rock platform, I was lifted up, as if by an invisible hand, and placed on its surface. Now the lamb was right beside me. Carefully, I set down Hope's egg.

"May I see your mouth?" I asked.

The lamb stood as still as if it had been carved out of wood. Arm dripping with water, I reached toward its face.

From between its teeth, I pulled out a coin.

It was the size of a dime. The silver was tarnished. A Roman emperor's face was on one side, a woman in a chair on the other. I stared at the coin for a long time. A part of me could not believe what I held.

"You found it," I told the lamb. "You found it. And then I found you."

"And then, lucky me," a voice said, "I found all three of you."

I didn't need to look to know who the speaker was. I could recognize that bitter, hate-filled voice with my eyes closed.

But look I did, and there he was, standing at the edge of the pool. The golden rays that poured down from the cave's roof made him look wickeder than ever.

"Hello, Gordon," I said. My voice was calm.

Gordon smiled that ferocious smile of his.

The knife he held had a long, curved blade made of metal so shiny and sharp that it glowed.

Chapter 23

ordon looked filthy. His camouflage pants were covered in mud. His T-shirt was torn. His wild, unkempt hair was matted to his head, and his sideburns were caked with grime.

"Give me the coin," he snarled.

"No."

He laughed unhappily. Then he lifted his arm and forcefully sliced his knife blade through the air. There was a whizzing sound. A ripple spread across the pool's surface. "You stupid girl," Gordon said. He took a step into the water.

I didn't think. I just moved. I reached down, picked up Hope's egg, and threw. I watched the beautiful brown oval sail across the pool and hit Gordon square in the face.

He yelled. Then he dropped his knife into the water. And then he yelled some more as the egg yolk dripped down his nose.

"You think I can't take that coin from you bare-handed, little girl? I don't need a knife to wrestle you." He took another step. The water was up to his ankles.

I had been scared before, but never had I felt panic. That's the kind of fear that floods your brain, making it nearly impossible to think. I knew what Gordon said was true: He didn't need a knife to hurt me. He was a foot taller than me and at least twice my weight. There was no way I could fend him off on my own.

But I would try.

I made a choice. For Gabby's lamb, who was lost. For Crystal and her ruined mane. For Hope, who had finally laid an egg. For Simon and his busted lip. For Momma, drop-dead tired at the restaurant. And for Daddy, my big, strong daddy, who, if he were well, would have lifted Gordon up by his collar and shoved him against the cave wall.

"I am tough and brave," I had told Sister Melanie. Now it was time to prove those words were true.

There was only one problem: I had no idea what to do.

But *do* I must. Gordon was edging his way deeper into the pool.

"You think I can't swim?" he called. "You think I'm scared of a little cave water?"

It was hard to breathe. Every time I inhaled, it felt like only the slightest whisper of air entered my lungs. I was light-headed, too.

Don't you dare faint, Pet, I told myself, and shoved the coin into my pocket for safekeeping.

That's when I felt the smooth metal lid.

See, I'd forgotten, but all this time the saltshaker had been right there.

"You'll know when you need it," Sister Melanie had said when she gave it to me the morning of Simon's birthday. Truth be told, I didn't know if a saltshaker was what I needed right now, but I knew I needed something, and that little metal container was all I had.

"You better watch out!" I yelled. I tried to sound intimidating, but my voice, echoing in the cave, was high-pitched and hysterical, like a ridiculous bird's.

Gordon paid me no mind. He was up to his knees in the water.

"I warned you!" I shouted, and then I did the only thing you can do with a saltshaker. I shook it. Back and forth, up and down. I stood on the edge of the rock platform and shook out every single grain of salt. The grains fell into the water like snowflakes and instantly disappeared.

Gordon began to laugh, loud and cruel. "Is that all you got? You going to turn me into a French fry with your magic salt?"

My knees shook. I didn't know it was possible to feel so scared. But it wasn't just fear. There was disappointment, too. I don't know what I expected when I emptied the saltshaker, but I expected *something,* not the nothing I got. *Oh, Sister Melanie,* I wondered, full of desperation, *why would you play me for a fool?*

And it was at that moment that everything changed.

The light from above went from golden to gray. The pool morphed from clear and calm to a roiling blue as waves formed on its surface. Small and gentle at first, they began to grow, increasing in size and force. A sick feeling spread in my stomach. This was bad. Very bad.

"Gordon," I called to him over the lapping waves, "get out of the water."

Gordon's face was a mixture of confusion and rage. "What did you do?"

"I don't know."

The water was at his waist. The waves were big enough now to make a crashing sound when they rolled across the pool's surface.

Beside me, the lamb bleated. Then it pressed its soft muzzle against my knee.

"Gordon," I tried again, "I don't think you should be in there."

"Don't you, huh? You think I should be scared of a little water? Well, I got news for you: I don't care!"

And with those words, Gordon began to swim. His head bobbed precariously while the rest of his body was covered by the blue waves.

"Stop!" I cried. No longer was I afraid for myself—I was afraid for him. My enemy. The man who had hurt my brother, my pony, and threatened to stab me twice. I was afraid he would die. And a little lost lamb and I would be the only ones to witness his drowning.

"If you turn around, I'll give you half the coin's value!" I had to scream to make my voice heard over the crashing waves.

"Not half!" Gordon sputtered as the rough water tossed his body. "All!"

And then I cried because I could not give him all. I could not sacrifice my family for this man who refused to save himself.

The lamb bleated sorrowfully.

"All!" Gordon howled. And then it became his rallying cry. "All!" he'd yell, then a wave would crash over him, and his head would disappear underwater for a few seconds. The instant he resurfaced, the word would fly from his mouth. "All!"

Somehow, he was making his way across the pool. His face was red. His eyes looked rabid. The hot hatred burning inside him was acting like a propeller.

Up on the limestone platform, I pulled the lamb backward, against the cave wall. I had no plan for when Gordon reached us. I'd thrown the egg. I'd shaken the salt. There was nothing left.

That's what I thought.

But then there was a sound, like a great rushing of air. And a fish rose out of the water. The fish was enormous, big as a shark, and looked like something from dinosaur times. Its scales were bloody red, and it had yellow, goggling eyes. On top of its head were two long feelers, purple like bruises.

Gordon saw the fish—he had to have—but so consumed was he by the thought of the coin that he couldn't stop his cries. "All! I want it all!"

Slowly, the fish made its way to him. It opened its mighty jaws.

"All!" Gordon yelled as he swam into its mouth.

The fish snapped closed its jaws, blinked its yellow eyes, and sank back down into the water.

And then it and my enemy were gone.

Chapter 24

Everything changed. In the flip of a fin, the stamp of a hoof, the blink of an eye. When the fish disappeared, it all turned back to the bright before. Light spilled down, illuminating the cave in flecks of gold. The pool turned clear and calm. The lamb, whose wool was laced with silver, gracefully leapt into the water and swam to shore.

"*Baa,*" the magnificent creature called to me when safely on the other side.

I didn't hesitate, not for a moment. I jumped into the pool, and that same invisible hand glided me across the water.

And do you know what I thought of, after everything that had happened? With the rarest of coins in my pocket, dripping wet, standing in an enchanted cave? I thought of Simon. I wondered if he was awake now. Because if he was, he would be hungry. I wondered if I could find something to feed him.

So that's what I was thinking about—breakfast—as I followed the lamb out of the cave.

It wasn't dark anymore in the tunnels. The golden light now spread everywhere, showing the way. When we got to the entrance, the lamb turned around, as if to make sure I was still there.

"*Baa.*"

"Don't worry. I'm coming," I said, and then followed it down the steep incline into the forest.

At first, I thought the high-pitched fluttery sound was birds. A flock of sparrows maybe, in the distance. But the closer I got, the less birdlike the sound became, until I realized it was human. Voices, I mean. There were people at the campsite.

I began to run.

If there were people, that meant Simon and I were no longer lost. Maybe someone had come to lead us home. And then I couldn't help but think of breakfast again and all the pieces of cinnamon toast I'd make for Simon, stacked tall and buttery brown on a plate. But first I'd have him brush his teeth extra good, two times in a row, to make up for the times we missed.

When I came into the camp clearing, there was white cloth everywhere, and it took me a minute to realize what I was seeing. Then it hit me: nuns. Dozens of nuns. The sisters had come from the abbey.

One sat with Simon on a bench, feeding him a granola bar. Another stood beside Crystal, a hand on the pony's back as she grazed in the dewy grass. An old, round sister had Hope pressed against her broad chest, while the others stood some distance off, in a circle. I could hear their lilting voices, light and indistinct. I think they were praying.

The lamb went over to a sister not far from us and used its teeth to pull on the skirt of her robe. The young woman turned around and clasped her hands in delight at the beautiful creature. Then the nun saw me.

"Perpetua!" she cried, and came running, arms outstretched, red glasses bouncing on the bridge of her nose.

Then Sister Melanie's arms were around me before I could say as much as hello. Cheek pressed to her robe, I breathed in her clean summer scent. My throat felt swollen. I knew I could not speak, even if I wanted to. This sister who was not *my* sister, but whom I was somehow joined to nonetheless.

"You have been found, Perpetua," Sister Melanie whispered, and kissed the top of my head.

I pulled away from her when I realized how filthy I must be, since I couldn't even remember the day of my last shower. I didn't want to soil her white robe.

"A little dirt's never bothered me." She laughed. But by saying that she only confirmed how visibly grimy I was.

"What are you doing here?" I asked, and gestured with my good arm at all the sisters.

"Looking for you, of course." Sister Melanie laughed again.

"But how did you know I was lost?"

"Oh, Perpetua, all of Iowa knows you're missing."

I was confused, and my face showed it.

"When your mother found your letter, she called the police. There have been stories in the newspaper and on TV. Hundreds of people have been searching this valley the past two days."

I nodded and suddenly felt very small. I did not like to think of Momma with shaking hands dialing 911. I did not care to imagine Daddy's face when my name and picture flashed on the TV.

"We found a metal detector," Sister Melanie continued, "a backpack, and then your shoes." She glanced at my bare feet. "We were all terribly frightened that we could not find *you*.

"We broke into parties and searched from sunrise

to sunset. Dogs were brought to track your scent. But nothing. And then, early this morning, I was alone in the chapel, praying for your safe return and waiting for the sun to rise so we could once again begin the search. I was on my knees in front of the altar when all of a sudden I felt a presence. There, in the guest entrance, stood a woman holding a staff and dressed in a purple robe.

"'I've lost my lamb,' she said. 'Will you help me find it?'

"'Of course,' I said, 'when the sun rises.'

"'No, not then. Now. Come.'

"I tell you, Perpetua, for a moment I didn't know what to do. But then I ran to my superior to ask her permission. And she had the same feeling I did—that this was a most *unusual* situation. And I had another feeling I didn't dare speak: that good would come if I heeded the shepherdess's command.

"So Mother Superior and I gathered all the sisters who were physically able, and we went out into a day so new it was still dark. The shepherdess had a lantern, and that's what we followed, for she walked so quickly, it was impossible to keep up. Her purple robe was all but invisible in the darkness, but that burning light bobbed ahead in the distance.

"We walked for an hour, maybe two, and then we realized the sun had come up and the lantern had disappeared. And here we are." She gestured with her arms at the campsite.

"When you got here," I asked, "was Simon still sleeping?" That's something that had begun to gnaw at me—the idea of my baby brother waking up and finding himself all alone.

"Yes, but not for long. Twenty nuns stomping through a campsite make a lot of noise. Now I've said everything I can think of. Your turn, Perpetua. And first things first—what happened to your arm?" She frowned slightly and touched my silver bandages.

"I was trampled in a cattle stampede and broke a bone, but luckily a giant archer found me and wrapped it in disappearing cloth."

Sister Melanie looked at me a moment, and then she said very slowly, "Oh. But other than that you're all right?"

"Well, when Gordon stole his metal detector, Simon fell off the pony and busted his lip. But the shepherdess floated across the water and stitched him up with magic thread. Then Gordon came in the night and cut off the pony's mane and stole our backpacks. I thought we were going to starve—until we got caught in a rainstorm and discovered a man in a monster mask who lived in an enchanted cabin. I could barely think straight after the cow stampede, which is why I made a promise to Gordon, who pointed a knife in my face and stole my shoes."

I had to pause to catch my breath.

"But then the giant showed up and gave me the best broth I'd ever had in my life. When I woke up, the little lamb led me to a cave. Of course, Gordon found it, too, so I had to use the saltshaker to save us. Then I begged him not to swim across the rough waters, but he wouldn't listen. So a prehistoric fish ended up swallowing him whole. The lamb then led me back to the campsite, and here we are."

I made a motion toward the lamb, but it was nowhere to be seen. "Oh no. The lamb is lost again."

"That is quite the tale, Perpetua." Sister Melanie was quiet for a long time. Then she leaned toward me and whispered, "Were you able to find anything else? In addition to the lamb, I mean."

I slipped my hand into my pocket and pulled out the coin.

Sister Melanie gasped and brought her fingers to her mouth. Then she cried out, "Come, everyone. Come and see what Perpetua has found."

They came. Simon carried Hope. One nun led Crystal. And all the other white-robed sisters joined, too. They formed a semicircle around me.

"Behold Brother Brendan's coin," Sister Melanie announced, and I held it outstretched so they all could see.

There was a murmuring like the rustling of wings, and then all the nuns fell to their knees.

It was the strangest thing to stand in the woods like that, with all those women kneeling around me. *This is what it must feel like to be a queen,* I thought. And truth be told, it was not my favorite feeling.

Slowly the sisters stood up.

"Shall we take you home?" Sister Melanie asked.

"Cheese," Simon said immediately, before I had a chance to answer. Everyone laughed because *cheese,* of course, meant, "Yes, take me home right now, as fast as you can. What are you waiting for? Please hurry. Yes."

So we formed a procession. Simon sat atop the pony, crown on his head, scepter and chicken in his hands. Sister Melanie held Crystal's reins, and all the other nuns followed single file behind them. I was at the very front, the coin held straight out before me.

Why I was picked to be parade leader, I don't know, since I was the one who'd gotten us so lost it took the nuns two days to find us. But there I was, head of the pack. And here's one more mystery to join the dozen others: I led us right out of there. The coin pulled me forward like a dog straining at its leash. Through woods, across fields, dipping into valleys, until finally the farmhouse came into view.

"Cheese!" Simon cried triumphantly.

And my heart leapt in my chest. We did it. The impossible task had been completed. The coin that had been lost for generations had finally been found. And now we were back where we belonged, victory spoil in hand.

"*Veni, vidi, vici!*" I sang. I couldn't help myself. I felt like a general who'd just won a decisive battle.

I came, I saw, I conquered.

(With a little bit of help, of course.)

Chapter 25

We dropped Hope off at the henhouse. "You'd better start laying eggs," I told her when I set her down among the flock. "No more excuses. I know you can do it." I kissed the top of her soft, dusty head.

It was then that Sister Melanie told us what to expect.

"In the parking lot at the top of the hill," she said, "there is going to be a lot of commotion. Farmers, police officers, search dogs, TV news vans. I don't want to frighten you, Perpetua, but going up there as you are right now might be like stepping into a lion's den."

I looked at the coin, and I knew she was right. There were lots of Gordons in the world, lots of people who'd be willing to sacrifice everything—including their own bodies—in a mad quest to have it all. I put the coin in my pocket.

"That's not going to be enough," one of the nuns said.

"What do you suggest?" asked another.

"What they need are disguises," said a third.

Sister Melanie and the mother superior exchanged glances. Then each took off her robe and veil, revealing farm clothes—jeans, T-shirt, and a bandanna—underneath.

"Now, that's what I'm talking about," the third nun said.

"We are initiating you into the order." The mother superior laughed, and she slipped the robe over my body, then fastened the veil on my head. Sister Melanie did the same for Simon, after lifting him from the pony and removing his crown. And that is how my brother and I became the shortest, youngest Trappistine nuns in the history of Iowa.

"I'm not sure this will fool anyone," I whispered to Simon as we fell in place inside the circle of sisters. Then I had to bite the inside of my cheeks to keep from laughing because he looked so absolutely ridiculous in a robe long enough to be a wedding gown.

We walked up the hill to the parking lot. A crowd was waiting, as Sister Melanie had foretold. There were two police cruisers, a bright blue news van, and dozens of people wearing straw hats and backpacks.

"Anything?" someone in the crowd yelled.

The mother superior stepped forward. "Good news is imminent. I'm confident," she said. I'm not sure anyone recognized her, seeing as how she was dressed in blue jeans and a bandanna.

"Where'd you get that horse?" someone else asked.

"Hey, weren't the kids supposed to have stolen a pony?"

A police officer emerged from the crowd. "Ma'am, I'd like to have a word with you."

In the meantime, Sister Melanie had quietly separated from the group and was leading Crystal down the path that wound to the gravel road. She motioned for Simon and me to join her. And we did—without a single person trying to stop us.

When we reached the sign that marked the abbey's entrance, I said to Sister Melanie, "I can't believe we were able to walk away from that crowd. No one even seemed to notice."

"Many things that seem impossible are not. You of all people should know that, Perpetua."

"Please don't talk in riddles," I said a bit more crossly, a bit more Momma-like, than I had intended. Maybe I was tired. Maybe, now that we were so close, I was anxious to get home.

"It's not a riddle, just a fact. It's hard to see what you don't expect." And then she flashed a mysterious smile and set Crystal's reins in my hand. "Your parents are waiting for you. They were told to keep vigil at home in case you returned. So . . . *Vale*, Sister Perpetua. *Vale*, Sister Simon." She gave a slight bow and headed back down the abbey lane.

Simon and I, still dressed in our robes, began the short journey home.

The sun was high overhead, the sky as clear as the day we started out. And now that we were returning home, it almost seemed like we'd never left. Or maybe it seemed like everything that had happened hadn't really happened. Maybe it had all been a dream I'd been having, lying in my bed. How I wanted to slip a hand into my pocket, to feel the coin and prove its existence, but I couldn't because of the robe.

We came first to Holly's ramshackle house on the way to our own. He stood in the driveway, next to his pickup. When he saw us, he began to shout.

"Thieves!" he cried. "It's the thieves! The no-good child thieves have returned!"

His voice was as grumpy as ever, so I was surprised to feel a smile tug at the corners of my mouth. When his lanky frame had advanced near enough that he could hear me, I said: "Not thieves, just borrowers."

"Borrowers, my foot," he said, and grabbed Crystal's reins from my hand. "And look what you've done to her."

I looked again at her hacked-off mane, her stub of a tail. I touched her flank. "I'm sorry. I didn't mean for this to happen."

"You didn't mean to go wild on my pony with a pair of scissors?"

"I'm not the one who did it, sir," I said softly, "but I take full responsibility and will make it up to you somehow."

Holly grunted. Then he said bitterly, "*You* still have a nice long ponytail. Funny the scissors didn't come after *your* hair."

I cast my eyes to the driveway, kicked at the gravel with my bare toes. And I bit my tongue because I knew I deserved whatever unkindness he offered. I'd taken without asking and returned what I'd taken the worse for wear.

There was silence, and then Holly said, as if just noticing our attire, "So, what—you ran away to join the convent?"

"No, sir," I said. "We were looking for something."

"What?"

"Cheese," Simon said.

"Cheese? No need to steal a pony and run away from home in search of a piece of cheese. I'd have given you a whole block of the stuff if you'd asked. At least then Crystal would still have some hair."

I shot Simon a stern look. "It wasn't cheese, Mr. Hollis. It was something valuable."

The old man grunted again. "There ain't nothin' worth nothin' down at that abbey. Come on, Crystal," he said, and led her back toward the barn.

Simon and I continued, neither of us speaking, down the road.

My heart skipped a beat when it came into view: our farmhouse, white and a little bit weathered, but absolutely perfect under the bright summer sun with Daddy's wood carvings dotting the yard.

As we got closer, I could see two figures, side by side on the front-porch swing, right next to our family statue. I knew who they were, of course—Momma and Daddy—but the sight stopped me in my tracks. The two of them hadn't sat together like that since Daddy fell. To see them now was almost like traveling back in time, to the better before.

I looked at Simon and gave him a nod, and then we both started to run. Oh, how the gravel stung my bare feet, but I didn't care. My brother and I ran, veils flapping, robes twisting. I don't know how we didn't fall. I guess that's just one more miracle to add to the list.

We were so close now I could read the numbers on our mailbox. Momma and Daddy caught sight of us and stood.

"Simon? Pet?" my momma's voice, part scared, part hopeful, called.

And then my feet touched the grass of my own front yard, and it was like fireworks in my heels. Momma ran, too, with Daddy right behind her.

"Simon! Pet!"

It wasn't a question anymore but an exclamation.

And you know how before, the important moments would slow down? Well, this moment sped up so fast that I could hardly tell what was happening. Next thing I knew, Momma's arms were around Simon and me, and she was smooshing us together while pressing us to her chest.

"My kids. My kids," she repeated, and as she did, her tone switched back and forth between fury and joy. "Don't you ever do that again."

Tears streamed down her cheeks, and she didn't bother to wipe them away. I don't know if you've ever made your mother cry, but when it happens, you feel about an inch tall, and there's nothing in the world you wouldn't promise to make her stop.

"We won't, Momma. We won't."

Then she let go. I felt almost naked without her embrace, standing there, facing my daddy. There were no tears on his cheeks. His dark brown eyes looked sad, though. And suddenly I felt like I hadn't seen him in months. I missed him something fierce, even though he stood right in front of me.

"You can't begin to fathom how worried we've been," he said.

"I know." I looked at his arm, all useless and hanging there. And I thought of my own useless arm. We were mirror images, he and I. The thought was so sad that I burst into tears and ran and pushed my face into his big, broad chest.

"Oh, Pet," he whispered. I felt his hand on my back. "I'm glad you're home."

There was silence. I breathed in the familiar smell of wood shavings on his shirt. Somehow his clothes still smelled of sawdust even though he hadn't picked up a chain saw in months.

"Why are my children dressed up like nuns?" Momma finally asked. It was such an absurd question that we all laughed.

"It's a long story," I said.

Momma helped us out of our veils, then removed our robes. Daddy's eyes immediately fell on my silver bandages. "Your arm," he said.

"Don't worry. Everything will be okay." I reached into my pocket and pulled out the coin.

Momma didn't know what it was, since she was from California. But Daddy, who had grown up here, he knew. He took it from my fingers. His hand trembled. With his thumb and forefinger, he held the coin up to his face in wonder.

"In all my wildest dreams," he said, his voice almost a whisper.

Simon clapped his hands in delight and began to jump up and down.

"What is it?" Momma asked.

"It's—it's—" But Daddy couldn't finish.

There wasn't a cloud in the sky, and how that sun shone down on us. Its rays were majestic, lighting up the whole earth. Everything they touched sparkled: Daddy's hair, his beard, and, of course, the coin.

I had never seen a more beautiful picture in my life than my daddy right then, so awash in wonder that he couldn't speak. It filled my heart with a joy so big and powerful I thought it would burst.

"What is it?" Momma asked again.

Simon opened his mouth. His eyes caught mine. They sparkled with mischief, like in the old days.

I knew what he was going to say, of course. "Cheese." Our daddy, according to Simon, was holding the most wonderful piece of cheese. And then we'd all laugh.

But that is not what Simon said.

Simon opened his mouth, and what he said was this: "It's a coin, Momma. Pet found it. Now we shall all be saved."

Chapter 26

I'm going to tell you how it all turned out. That way you don't have to guess. I hate guessing how a story ends. Don't you?

Simon started talking again, which I suppose is obvious. He picked up right where he'd left off when Daddy fell. And he talked, and he talked, and he talked. He talked so much that sometimes I missed the days when he would only say *cheese*. Just kidding.

Sort of.

A visit to the emergency room revealed my arm was broken in three places. I got to wear a hot-pink cast that stretched all the way from my shoulder to my wrist. It looked pretty cool—and all the nuns signed it—but, oh, was it sweaty and gross in July and August.

Crystal's hair grew back. It was silkier and blonder than ever. It took me a while to think of a way to make amends for borrowing her without permission. But finally I thought of a plan. I mucked her stall—and all the other ponies'—free of charge for the rest of the summer.

Hope never did lay another egg. "I guess that one was a fluke," I told Sister Melanie.

"Not a fluke, but a gift," she corrected, because I'd told her how Hope had laid it just in time for me to throw it at Gordon.

Well, whatever the egg was, fluke or gift, we all still loved that unfruitful little chicken just the same.

Speaking of Gordon—whom I try not to even *think* about, let alone say his name—he was never seen again. I'm sure that doesn't surprise you, seeing as how he was swallowed by a giant fish—but other people—specifically the grown-ups—couldn't seem to wrap their minds around that fact. There were search parties and missing posters on grocery-store bulletin boards for a long time.

I don't know how his mother, Mrs. Minnow, felt about his absence. I'm sure she was sad, because mothers love their children, regardless of whether they're good or bad. When Simon and I visited her, though, she never mentioned him, and I saw her shed no tears. She still gave us each a bag of vanilla wafers, but now that Gordon was gone, she hardly ever said, "Oh dear."

We still haven't found Gabby's lamb, but I guess that's okay because we haven't seen Gabby—or Mike or A.R.—either. If I didn't know better, I might think I'd imagined them. Sister Melanie has tried several times to retrace the path she took the morning she followed the lantern. But the cave seems to have vanished.

Somehow, word leaked about our discovering the coin. Those first days back, there was a slew of reporters parked on our front lawn. A picture of our house was even shown on cable TV. Everyone wanted to interview me or at the very least take a picture of the coin. But Momma taped a note to our front door that read: *We are talking to no one and showing you nothing.* We kept the curtains drawn and the doors shut and didn't dare stick so much as a toe outside for three whole days. When the reporters saw Momma was serious, they packed up their cameras and went home.

To say there was a lot of interest in the coin would be an understatement. We got calls from collectors, kings, and CEOs. The plan was to have an auction in New York City and sell it to the highest bidder, but then Sister Melanie and the mother superior showed up one evening with an enormous basket of taffies and a proposal of their own.

They said they wanted to purchase the coin from us, to put on display in the chapel for the whole world to see. And while they could not match what a king or businessman might offer, they were willing to pay handsomely for it out of their candy reserves.

Later that night, Momma and Daddy called me to the kitchen table.

"Since you are the one who found it, Pet," Momma said, "your father and I think it only fair that you should choose whom we sell it to."

"Nuns or New York?" Daddy asked. His eyes were steady and oh so brown. "You don't have to decide right now. If you need time to think . . ."

But I didn't need time to think. I knew my answer as soon as he asked the question. I had no allegiance to wealthy collectors, but the nuns who had found Simon and me and ensured our safe return home—well, they were like sisters.

"Nuns," I said.

Momma blinked.

"That's my girl," said Daddy.

Once we had the money, Momma didn't have to work so much anymore. She was a thousand times nicer when her feet didn't hurt. And though I love my momma even when she's mean, I love her more when she's not.

Arriving home from school one day, I found her seated at the kitchen table.

"What are you doing?" I asked.

"Planning," Momma said. "Look what came in the mail."

I stepped closer. A seed catalog was spread open in front of her.

"Spring will be here before you know it," she said. "Would you like to help me choose what to plant?"

"Oh, Momma," I said, a love most wild and warm filling my chest, "there's nothing in the world I'd rather do than choose with you."

I ran and got a pen and a notebook, and we sat together for two hours, till we had a list of seeds four pages long.

Daddy had his surgery, and just like Momma had predicted all those months ago, the third time was a charm. His shoulder reattached. After many weeks of physical therapy, he was finally able to hold a chain saw.

Fair season had passed by then. The air had grown cold, and we had our first snow. So Daddy worked on his ideas inside. He put up a bulletin board and filled it with sketches of all the things he'd create once the weather warmed. There were drawings of chickens, and lambs, and an enormous prehistoric fish. But this was my favorite drawing of all: a little boy wearing a crown and holding a scepter, sitting atop a pony, with a tough, brave-faced girl in the front, leading them.

"Make that one first," I begged when I saw it.

My daddy laughed, and even though I'm eleven and too old to be carried, he scooped me up and held me tight in his two big, strong arms.

"Your wish is my command, Pet."

A million sunny days stretched like dominoes in his deep brown eyes.

Acknowledgments

That this book exists feels nothing short of miraculous. I'd like to express my gratitude to those who helped these pages materialize.

Enormous thanks to my amazing literary agent, Kerry Sparks, who guided the book to publication, thereby making one of my longest-held dreams come true.

At Random House Children's Books, Caroline Abbey was the first champion of my work, and later, Diane Landolf's editorial expertise helped polish it. Thank you both for your commitment.

Simon's condition was my own invention, but I'm indebted to Anu Subramanian for her professional thoughts.

My four children love books as much as I do, so it was a delight to read the first draft of this novel aloud to them. Thank you, Nolte kids, for taking such joy in words—especially your mother's.

And to Mike, my husband: You've always, from the very start, sacrificed your time so I'd have more of my own. Over and over, you encouraged me to seek the treasure. Well, I finally found the coin—and I'm so grateful you were beside me on the journey.